The Discontinuity of Small Things

The Discontinuity of Small Things

Kevin Haworth

Quality Words In Print

The Discontinuity of Small Things
a novel

Published by Quality Words In Print, LLC
P. O. Box 2704, Costa Mesa, California 92628-2704
www.qwipbooks.com

First Edition

Cover and Interior Design by Desktop Miracles, Inc.

Library of Congress Cataloging-in-Publication Data

Haworth, Kevin, 1971–
The discontinuity of small things /
by Kevin Haworth.— 1st ed.
p. cm.
ISBN 0–9713160–4–X
1. Denmark—History—German occupation, 1940–1945—Fiction. 2. World War, 1939–1945—Denmark—Fiction. 3. Jews—Denmark—Fiction.
I. Title.
PS3608.A895D57 2005 813'.6—dc22
2004004519

Printed in the United States of America

"Wherever I go,
I am always
Traveling toward Jerusalem."

Rebbe Nachman of Bratslav

For Zev and for his Ema

Author's Note

This is the history of Denmark during the war years as it has occurred to me. The places are actual; the characters are imagined; the events of the novel take both fact and fiction into account.

For their encouragement and support during the writing of this book I thank my editor Holly Gruber; my teachers and colleagues at Arizona State University, the Vermont Studio Center, and The Shefa Fund; and most especially, my large and loving family.

Thanks to the Rabbi Morris N. Kertzer Memorial Scholarship at Arizona State University and to the Vermont Studio Center for supporting portions of the research and writing.

Part One

occupation

1

to dream the dream of Jerusalem

Rain from the sky in the form of paper. All morning a flurry of pulp and pressed ink has fallen out of a grey sky. The papers are damp and salt-crusted from the sea air and they stick to Bakman's ankles as he walks.

It is Copenhagen, 1943.

He walks alone, witnessed only by a series of tight row houses and empty window boxes. A lone man, of average height, in worn clothes and glasses, with a piece of paper stuck to his ankle. These streets used to be clean, he thinks. The tall row houses lean over him as he walks down the street, hunched in his coat, shaking his leg to remove one of the damp pamphlets from his pant cuff. His grandmother would be horrified at these conditions. Seeing these conditions, she would sit at her large wooden desk and with a pen still fed by an inkwell she would direct a letter to the mayor's offices. It would be a charming letter. It would eviscerate the mayor in the most charming of ways. His grandmother knew the exact temperature to serve tea in the morning and the exact temperature to serve tea in the afternoon. She knew that a woman was not to be seen beyond her own bedroom in clothes that hadn't been washed and pressed and she knew the benefits of civic virtue. But his grandmother is dead. And civic virtue, if it ever existed, existed only in the parlor rooms of the homes of women like her. Bakman has heard—where he has heard he can't quite remember, it falls from the sky this information, it comes like a change of weather—that there are places in Europe where Jews clean the streets. Dragged from their shops, scrubbing the pavement on their hands and knees. Not in Denmark, of course. These things would never happen in Denmark. He looks at the street ahead of him, grey from soot and littered with paper.

As Bakman walks the events of that morning come back to him. He tries to put them off again, concentrating instead on the rain and on the occasional flowerbed, window box, man sweeping his doorway. There are things you don't talk about. Up ahead where it's busier he'll turn right. He can see a couple of people hurrying along, but the usual grey-uniformed presence on the street corner missing. At least the rain keeps the German soldiers inside.

But of course it is not really rain.

Bakman turns onto a winding street that leads to the harbor. A well-dressed couple walks past him. The woman throws him a strange look, then leans over and laughs something into her partner's ear. Bakman looks down at his shoe, sees the pamphlet stuck to the heel. He stops, balances on one leg like an awkward bird, tries to kick it off. But that doesn't work, so he reaches across with one hand, hopping, switching hands, swipes at his foot on its way down like some excited Russian dancer. Finally. But he's only succeeded in transferring it to his palm and he shakes that as if a cockroach has descended from his sleeve. Other pedestrians walk around him, staring and giggling. He drops his hand to his side, stares back, reaches over with the free one to peel off the pamphlet. It reads, in bad Danish:

> Continue your faith in der Führer. The historic union between Germany and Denmark will withstand unprovoked attacks from the British, the Jews, and other undesirables. Heil hitler!

He drops that pamphlet into the street; picks off another one that has fastened itself to his left pant leg. It reads, also in bad Danish:

> Freedom soon. Place candles in windows tonight as a sign of support for the allied effort.

So you can see where to bomb us? Bakman thinks. At least you could take the time to write to us with proper grammar. But no, not here. We're not important enough. Sometimes, when the sky is clear, he can see the German and British planes, with their competing markings, flying high above the Copenhagen buildings, belching their leaflets on the city. High up, in the thin air, the pilots circle, their leather helmets buckled down and their goggles adjusted. They know just how to ignore each other. They know that they don't waste bullets on each other, not over Denmark. It's a psychological war they're having here, Bakman thinks. We're losing.

He follows the winding streets that lead to the harbor, the papers still fluttering down, but more slowly now, dropping like the last snowfall of the year. He turns a corner and he's arrived, at the Nyhaven harbor, at the water. The groaning of the boats as they rub against the dock. The worn, once brightly colored row houses that line the water's edge, leaning forward for the best view of the ocean. Bakman has long wanted an apartment down here, with a view of the water; he looks into the windows above him and tries to catch glimpses of a potential life. But he can't afford it. He has a cheap boarding-house room in the hospital's worst neighborhood. There's something in the salt air down here that moves him, that makes him think of places past the ocean, whereas his sweaty room only reminds him of long hours, fitful sleep, and shoddy wet dreams. He could never afford a place down here on his tiny medical student's stipend. So instead he misers his money and comes once a week to a café next to the water.

This café didn't have a view of the water directly—except for a seat far in the corner that was difficult to get to—but it was close, achingly close. The shop drew an odd clientele, slumming university students mixed with fishermen whose sea smell had burrowed into the café's walls and tables, the students coming to escape the university, the fishermen coming simply because the place was only a few steps from their boats.

As Bakman approaches he is met by a sign out front: SORRY, NO MILK TODAY. He almost laughs. TODAY. As if there might be milk tomorrow. As if there were milk yesterday. As if every table in Denmark had had fresh milk on it every day for the past three years.

It is the middle of the day, the only other customers a couple of out-of-work fishermen still in their heavy winter sweaters. They take no notice of Bakman. He sits. At least here he doesn't have to deal with the German soldiers, their brooding presence, the way everyone walked around them—they shunned this place because the café owner was Jewish. They didn't bother even to stand in front of the shop and glare the customers away, like they did at some Jewish-owned businesses. Bakman didn't know why they made the effort; business was bad everywhere in Denmark now.

He is served coffee without enthusiasm by a woman he has never seen before, even though he comes here once a week. The fishermen at the nearby table lean close to each other, their conversation foreign and imperceptible. Bakman wipes his glasses on his shirt, the lens a crosshatch of scratches like a child's drawing. He needs new ones, of course, but they can't be purchased now, not at any price Bakman could afford.

He sips his coffee slowly, trying to make the one cup last. Henrik would have come by now, if he were coming. Henrik was supposed to meet him here. He was supposed to bring the pretty nurse with the round face—what was her name? Marina? Maria?—who Bakman had tried to approach at the hospital but had no luck with each time. He thought maybe here, where he was comfortable. He takes out his pocket watch, an old model with no backing, the tiny moving parts all clicking forward exposed to the air. If they haven't come by now, he thinks, they're probably not coming, not after the events of that morning.

A man had come into the emergency room at Bispebjerg Hospital where Bakman and Henrik, his friend and fellow medical student, served their rotations. The man looked typically Danish, blond-white hair, handsome, but he stared over Bakman's shoulder at something too distant to see. A friend was with him, also blond but not as handsome, and the friend said, There's been an accident. What kind of accident? Bakman said, but the friend put his hands up, palms forward, as if to say, No, that's all I have for you, and backed out the door still holding his hands out and then turned and ran. And then the handsome man with the strange look had pulled away his jacket to reveal a large, bloody wound on his right side, just below his ribs. He was pressing a piece of burlap over it with his hand but the burlap had already turned wet and brown and had fallen concave where the actual hole was. Henrik reached out quickly, pulling the man to a table and attempting to stanch the bleeding but the man expired almost as soon as he reached a reclining position. And Bakman had stood there unable to move at the sight of that horrendous wound.

It seemed afterward that Henrik had looked at the two men—the dying man and his fleeing friend—as if he knew them, but why would he? and he denied ever seeing them before. And when Henrik reached into the open cavity of the dead man and pulled out a piece of metal the size of Bakman's fist—a gnarled and jagged section of train track—he didn't note it on the corpse's paperwork, as was procedure, but dropped it into the pocket of his lab coat as if it were another hospital instrument that had wandered off from its proper place. Bakman had wanted to question Henrik about it then but there wasn't the opportunity, and now, with all the commotion and extra forms to fill out and chance for Henrik to stay after his shift and brag about his quick reactions to all the female members of the staff Bakman wouldn't get an opportunity to question Henrik or even to talk to the pretty nurse.

As Bakman reaches down to finish his coffee he feels someone standing near him. It's the café owner, a thin, greying man with a prominent Adam's apple, a feature that distracts Bakman every time he sees the man, the Adam's apple like an enlarged golf ball lodged in the man's throat, bobbing up and down when he speaks as if it were trying vainly to work itself free. He is standing off to the left and behind Bakman's shoulder. After a moment Bakman realizes the café owner is waiting for him to look up and recognize his presence so that a conversation might comfortably begin. They are not friends by any loose definition of that word. They are customer and proprietor. On a couple of previous occasions they have played chess but the café owner played badly and Bakman beat him easily so Bakman has avoided it since. The area in front of the café is empty and in the distance boats can be heard straining against their moorings. Bakman looks up.

Mr. Bakman? the café owner says, the golf ball quivering in his throat. Bakman nods hello. If it's possible to win a war through excessive politeness, Bakman thinks, we'll do it. He can picture the top officials of the Foreign Ministry after the invasion standing with their hats at waist level in front of an array of German colonels and asking, Please, would you mind leaving our little country, if it isn't too much trouble? And remaining as surprised as anything when it didn't happen.

How is the coffee? the owner offers, bowing his head slightly.

Fine, Bakman says. Since they both know it isn't really coffee and it isn't really fine, there doesn't seem any reason to discuss it further. The café owner asks about Bakman's family. Bakman replies too quickly that he has no family left—he's told the café owner this before.

Ah, the old man says. The golf ball hiccups in the throat. Of course.

Bakman would rather think about the pretty nurse with the round face and what she might look like with the top button of her uniform unfastened but it's impossible with this man standing next to him. I should be getting back to the hospital, Bakman says.

Yes, the café owner says. But he continues to stand there. The café owner seems ready to say something, and Bakman is afraid it's going to be terribly personal. From the corner of his eye he sees Henrik walking up the street. He turns to the café owner as if to say, See, I've got business to attend to. But the café owner is already gone, and so Bakman is left sitting there, waiting for Henrik as if he has nothing better to do. Which is true.

When Henrik sits down it's clear that he's brought nothing with him, neither the pretty nurse nor an explanation for that morning. When the waitress brings him his coffee, he winks at her. She smiles back at him.

Well? Bakman says.

Well, what? Henrik answers. He sips his coffee, grins at the waitress standing at the counter as if it's the best thing he's tasted all week.

Bakman looks at the empty chair at their table, the one that's supposed to be occupied by the nurse, then looks back at Henrik. She was busy, Henrik says, which Bakman interprets to mean, I haven't decided yet if I'm going to sleep with her first.

Fine, Bakman says. Why don't you explain to me what happened this morning?

What do you mean?

What do I mean? You know exactly what I mean.

Your voice is getting loud, Henrik says. You may not want that.

Bakman looks around, sees the fishermen in the corner looking at him.

Why don't you just explain to me what happened, then? Bakman says, leaning over the table.

I have no idea what you're talking about, Henrik says. He looks into his coffee cup, fishes something out with his finger. He inspects it for a moment, then flicks it away.

I saw you. I saw you put that scrap of metal in your pocket, Bakman says.

This pocket? Henrik asks, turning it inside out as if to say, See, nothing.

And what happened to that man? When I went to the morgue, afterwards, he wasn't there. Where did he go?

If you spent half as much time concerned with live patients as you did with dead ones, Henrik says, you'd be a much better doctor.

We're not finished with this, Bakman says.

Yes, we are, Henrik says. He leans over to Bakman, grabs him by the collar. The waitress, who had been walking toward them, turns and retreats back to the counter. Don't ask anything you don't want to know, Henrik hisses in Bakman's ear. Bakman pulls at his hand. Henrik lets go.

Don't sulk now, he says to Bakman. I'll get you that date with the nurse. Give it a couple of days.

Fine, Bakman says. And waves at the waitress to take their cups away.

A ship arrives in Copenhagen harbor. Twenty-six days ago it was called *The Sprite.* It steamed out of Newfoundland in cold weather, one of sixteen ships with weapons-quality scrap metal in its hold. The convoy set out into the North Sea, guarded by a single Canadian destroyer formerly outfitted to dredge rivers. Three days into the ocean the convoy was set upon by a pack of U-Boats. Later, a crewman from the destroyer—plucked dripping and shivering from the

Atlantic—reported that he had never heard so much screaming, nor had he known that a ship could burn underwater.

The Sprite stumbled into Cardiff with only two of the original fifteen ships still in the convoy. After emptying its hold it turned north in search of new cargo, laboring to the Faeroe Islands in a fog so thick the ship steered into port by guesswork and each sailor working the deck thought himself alone, a ghost. In a pub frequented by black marketeers and homesick British officers, allegiances were traded and lost. *The Sprite* was whitewashed and restenciled *Erik of Pomerania.* The ship acquired a load of cod—later ground up and placed in children's lunches in Berlin—and the captain noted in his personal log a new destination: Danzig, via Copenhagen.

In the Copenhagen harbor known as Nyhaven, a man leaves the ship. He has a Northlander's pale skin, but his hair is black and curled, the color of a deep inkwell, a seal's iris. His face cannot be read for age. His homes, the Faeroes, are a collection of rocky and volcanic islands urged up by the North Atlantic and neglected since. Only seventeen of the twenty-two individual islands are inhabited. An additional two contain a population of wild sheep. In the Faeroe Island town of Tórshavn he had boarded the ship while the watchman slept away a headache. The watchman drooling and still holding a drained bottle of aquavit against his chest. Once on the ship the dark-haired man began shoveling great handfuls of cod into the hold, a job he performed so fluidly and without error that no other crewmen thought to wonder at his presence. That was eleven days ago.

Now the Faeroese steps off the *Erik* and into Copenhagen. Papers fall onto the wooden promenade. In truth he had never seen a German. In truth he did not know where Germany was. The only indications he had that a war existed were the restrictions on fishing and—one night while tossing his toilet water into the ocean—seeing in the distant waves the flickering eye of a periscope and a dark, heavy shape in the water below.

He walks through Nyhaven, the dank waterfront houses on his right side, and on the other, moored boats filling the canal like a flowerbed. Were he to speak to anyone here, his North Atlantic language would suggest a grandfather's pointless mumblings, a Viking folktale, seawater splashing against rocks. But not one word would be understood. So he does not speak. The street signs in Danish would present to him a problem but the fact is that he cannot read a letter in any language. He walks. He steps over the falling papers, as indecipherable to him as runes. He walks by a beggar whose hand, even in sleep, is curled out to receive change. He walks by a German soldier dodging the paper rainstorm in a doorway. He continues down the street and vanishes into the city.

Hannah Bergstrom stands on the wooden quay in Nyhaven surrounded by beggars, fishmongers, potato vendors. She has come to dream the dream of Jerusalem. She is nineteen, pretty, and Jewish. Her black hair pulled like a cap against her head.

Hannah is accustomed to feeling a part of her world, perhaps because her father operates a successful paper mill and they have always had money. Standing at the wooden pier, the tall, shabby row houses close behind her, she looks like one of Mary Willumsen's illicit photographs, taken at the Helgoland bathing establishment, twenty years before but only a few blocks from this place. Women facing the camera, naked or in their *underlinnen.* No shame. These same photographs later distributed for free or for a small coin at the Scala Book Kiosk; the photographer herself arrested, the negatives destroyed. Corruption of an image. The private forced into public view. Standing over the canal, Hannah seems lifted from one of these photographs unseen for twenty years, clothed only because of the unpleasant weather, the paper rainstorm, a brisk wind. I didn't force these women to pose, the photographer said to the judge, as the bailiff smashed her camera. They wanted to. They wanted to take their clothes off.

Twenty minutes before. Hannah in a lecture hall at the university. It's a special Sunday lecture, only for advanced students, and in the summer no less. Just five years ago such a thing would have been impossible. But this is Copenhagen. Very modern.

The lecture hall is a wide, vacant room with few students, and Hannah feels small within it. The subject is Scandinavian Drama. Hannah tries to focus on the figure of the professor, gripping the lectern as if it were one of his intellectual enemies. For him, the students are irrelevant, faceless, sent here by Christensen, that pandering bastard, who was made chairman of the Drama department—the professor's own deserved position, as everybody knows—a position that Christensen stole from him with his cheap, popular theories and his weak, handsome jaw, and his entourage of simple, sycophantic students who wrote letters denouncing the professor as a Communist and a boor. And he grips the lectern with renewed fervor, now preparing to make another indisputable point, curls of boredom and derision on the students' faces, yes, but all part of Christensen's plot to derail him, and he won't be held back, until! A woman stands up in the fourteenth row! More Christensen! And she gathers her belongings as if she would leave in the middle of his lecture. And all the students see her, this young woman with the thick, black hair, there's no avoiding it, and the professor knows that if he can summon the right remark just at this moment, something witty, or stern, and plant that woman back in her seat he will have wrested the students away from Christensen and back into the admiration of his articles and essays where they belong.

But the remark doesn't come. And the black-haired woman walks down her aisle and past him—slowly, it seems to the professor, so deliberately slowly—while the professor can only watch, and it is only after she has disappeared from the lecture hall altogether that he can recapture his thoughts and return to Ibsen's narrative intentions. But by then the students have begun to completely ignore him and the professor can hear the sound of Christensen—that idiot!—laughing at him from his grand chairman's office two floors above.

Hannah flees the lecture hall, her coat and notebook gathered hurriedly to her hip, past the stern portraits of decades of scholars lining the halls. She couldn't take this back. There were not many women matriculated at the university generally, and this act, she knew, also served to reinforce the faculty's image of women as flighty and unsuitable for serious subjects.

Hannah steps out of the university building, into the fluttering papers falling out of the sky. She takes a moment to adjust her coat, settle her belongings. Things would be different now. There was no doubting that. Not just because she had quit her university class in the middle of a lecture, though she felt herself to be a serious young woman and the act was uncharacteristic of her—but because now, from Denmark, in a country heavy with the presence of German soldiers, it was possible for a Jew to reach Palestine.

Hannah has proof of this in her coat pocket. An envelope, twice smuggled to reach her hand, bearing a postmark of a place that existed two thousand years ago and then not again until it was rebuilt out of the desert, a sandy mirage, sixteen years earlier. Petaq Tiqva. Like other desert names then unknown but soon to become famous in the history of the world.

Why her? Hannah had wondered when the letter appeared in her mail. She hardly knew the author. She had been sitting with her mother in the bright, open front room of the family house in Bellahøj. Her mother had held the letter up to the light, looking at its foreign stamp, before handing it to Hannah. Who's this from? she had asked, and Hannah had replied, with perfect truthfulness, I don't know.

Later she discovered that she did know. Sofie Østenmuller was the daughter of a lawyer, Laurits Østenmuller, a pompous man with a pompous name, and like Hannah's father a member of the Jewish Businessmen's League. She and Sofie had been forced playmates while their parents socialized in their downstairs parlor, Sofie's candy-sticky hands roaming over Hannah's dolls, books, dresses. Her little brother Isaac sitting on his fat diapered bottom in the middle of her room and crying. Even as they became teenagers, cut their hair, bought fancy shoes, Hannah couldn't stop thinking of Sofie that way—as a sticky-fingered, awkward girl with a mouth full of chocolate. Their parents grew to see each other less often. Østenmuller's clients had deserted him—but the 1930's were hard on everyone, weren't they? And then, in the space of a single, hot afternoon, Sofie, Isaac, the entire Østenmuller family—had disappeared, taking only a few suitcases.

Now Hannah holds the letter Sofie has written from a kibbutz in Palestine. Paper falls from the sky. The first paragraph of Sofie's letter is brief; it says only *I have arrived,* along with some small talk about eating tomatoes and cucumbers at breakfast. But it's done its job, because here Hannah is, standing at the docks, in a neighborhood she would never come to otherwise, pulled down here by the long reach of a girl she hardly knows and has never particularly liked. She'll be soaking wet by the time she gets home. She'll be drenched to her underwear, her light blue school coat dotted grey with rain and her hair a matted mess, and besides suffering a strange look from the maid she'll have to conjure an explanation for her mother, who'll be waiting for her at the mahogany table with the tea set ready, and the only explanation she will have is the letter in her hand and that will explain nothing.

Behind her a fish vendor and a potato seller have started an argument, their voices harsh and threatening. Hannah takes a step closer to the water. The vendors' argument pulls the German soldier from his doorway. His uniform gives off a cordite-and-laundry smell. She has nowhere to go, the water on one side and now this argument on the other. Ignore them, her father had said about the Germans. They have their rules and we have ours.

More German soldiers arrive, like congregating moths, three now instead of just one. The fish vendor and the potato seller are not deterred. There is the matter of space. The seller who moves his cart back ten feet chances half a day's income. Hannah hears the click of a gun. She turns to the water. Better not to look. She hears the pattering of Danish policemen. One of the other shopkeepers must have called them. They have jurisdiction here. It is a fact well established. A brief discussion ensues, the German soldiers in their broken, bullying Danish, the local policemen muted but insistent. They agree to take away both vendors. There is begrudging assent by the soldiers. And when Hannah looks, a moment later, there is only open sidewalk where the entire incident had originated, a flurry of fallen papers in the space where the vendors' carts had stood. A few moments after, a new fish vendor and potato seller have emerged from the alleyways to take the place of the original ones.

Hannah turns back to the water and tries to find again the dream of Palestine. She knows that this is not an original dream. She knows that it is a dream assembled piece by piece, glued together like potshards. She knows that even her father says at the end of Passover Seder *Next Year in Jerusalem* but he doesn't really mean it and she thinks maybe she does. The salt air scratches her throat. A storm is blowing in off the water—she's watched it gather for the last fifteen minutes—real rain and not just paper and she feels alone and vulnerable at the water's edge. A real storm always seems to follow the papers, Hannah thinks, as if the flying planes provoked some response from the sky. She looks again at the grey water, the row houses that run right up to the water's edge, and tries to imagine Jerusalem. There's a painting, a version of that famous city, in a gilt frame above the dining room table of her parents' house in Bellahøj. It's a family heirloom, done by a Christian painter of minor reputation. By his hand Jerusalem has the shape of a medieval European city, with high stone walls and thatched roofs and peasants walking humbly down its streets. And behind Hannah the fish vendors and the shopkeepers continue their business as they always have although they also now accept German marks.

2

to crush an apparent weed

The fisherman's church at Gilleleje is a white cylinder topped by a cone of thatch and sits on a small rise overlooking the beach. It's a round church of the kind found throughout Denmark and across the water in Sweden. A graveyard marks out three sides of the church, stopping only where the grass ends and the rocky beach begins.

Twenty families sit in the church this Sunday listening to the itinerant Lutheran pastor, who serves each of the Sjælland fishing towns once every three weeks. In between he visits widows and the bedridden and conducts a well-known but whispered courtship with a woman in Hornbæk ten years older than himself. In the back of the church children giggle quietly and only once does a woman turn to shush them. Though the pastor lectures this morning on the precise relationship of God to the surrounding heavens, Gilleleje is a fishing town, and the families in church remain rooted to more earthly—and watery—concerns: the number of fish in last night's nets, whether the storm that dumped rain on Copenhagen that morning will climb to this part of North Sjælland. It hasn't so far, and for that, if for no other reason, the families in church are thankful.

Carl Jensen sits stiffly because the low wooden pew hurts his back. His back hurts nearly all the time now. He doesn't tell this to his wife, Jette, but she knows. She notes both the way he eats his soup, with one elbow levered to the table as support, and his new habit of sleeping on his side, facing away from her, as if to prevent even the slightest jostle. Jette runs her hand once through her husband's hair. In the twenty-four years of their marriage she sees that his face has aged—grown cracks and worry lines—but his hair has not: it remains as fine and blond as when he first came to work on her father's boat, when she was only fourteen. In church today the part-time pastor, who looks young and too gaunt to Carl, quotes Job—*See, I am of small worth, what can I answer You?*—and Carl ponders this question while also considering the split board on his fishing skiff that needs re-patching. Outside the weather is clear and brisk. From the Gilleleje church it is faster to reach several towns in Sweden than any significant part of Denmark. Even Helsingør is outside my usual boundary, Carl thinks, even though it sits only a few miles down the coast from Gilleleje.

It is Carl and Jette's habit after services have finished and after sharing a sip of coffee with the other families to walk through the Viking graveyard, located on a low hill set apart from the church cemetery. From the Viking graveyard Carl can see the Sound, the harbor where he lashes his boat, the church, the small collection of houses, all of Gilleleje, a modest sight. Squinting, Carl can discern the train station to the south and west that connects Gilleleje to the other fishing towns, to Sjælland, to Denmark, and from there to all the wide continent of Europe at war.

Jette sits and unwraps a piece of cheese and coarse bread while Carl wanders among the graves. They have no children. After her third miscarriage Carl refused to try again, seeing what little he possessed lessen with each rush of blood down her legs.

Carl doesn't tend the Viking graves, exactly; certainly not the way that Anders Mortensen dresses his mother's buryplace in the nearby Christian cemetery, pulling masses of dandelions on his hands and knees, scraping mites from the flower petals, straightening crosses that the wind has tilted. But Carl does, as he wanders, sometimes reach out with his large boot to crush an apparent weed. Each Viking grave is a series of broken stones, chipped at the top and pointed like molars. They sketch out the closed curve of a Viking longship, the prow of each grave pointed toward the rock-strewn beach and past that, to the rough water of the Sound. There are seventeen in all. They are nameless for the simple reason that not one of the Vikings could read.

Carl looks up to see the pastor walking up the hill. The pastor has a young, earnest face and a habit, when conversing with his congregants, of tilting his head in what seems to Carl an exaggerated version of listening.

Still, the man is sincere enough, and Carl is not hostile to his company.

When the pastor reaches the Viking graveyard he pauses to pull out a small wooden cross and pass it over the Viking graves, all the while mumbling a short repetition of certain Psalms. The pastor always performs this act when visiting Carl and Jette up here, though for whom the young man seeks blessing in this spot—the Vikings' or their own—Carl can't determine. Likewise the nature of his prayers, penitent or punitive.

When he finishes the pastor stows the cross in his black peacoat and looks at them. Jette, he says, and nods. Then he looks at Carl.

I'll come right to the point, he says. Jette has spoken to me about something. It is about the possibility of her leaving Gilleleje.

Go on, Carl says.

Your wife has expressed a desire to move to Copenhagen. Her sister lives there, is that correct?

Yes, Carl says.

And you?

I do not wish it, he says, surprising even himself with the hardness of his response. He turns to Jette, but her head is down and she looks at the folds of her skirt as if to find something there.

I want you to understand that I would be sad to see you go, the pastor says. You have a place here. But when Jette tells me about her desire I must hear it. That is all I have come to say.

Won't you take a bite of cheese and bread, Jette says to him, holding it out. No thank you, the pastor says. I have already eaten. Then he turns and descends to the church. To other ministry.

Carl bends to pick a weed from the Viking grave nearest his boot. He is thinking now of a thing this same young pastor said to him two years ago, when the clergyman first arrived in Gilleleje. The part-time pastor, noting that all the stone graves pointed east, suggested one afternoon to Carl that the pagan Vikings somehow anticipated Jerusalem. Idol-worshippers and indiscriminate throat-cutters in life, in death they sought Our Lord. No, Carl replied. He watches his wife tie the bundle of bread and cheese. The wind is blowing toward him and he can smell the cheese wrapped in the salt air. He loves his wife's body, her white skin and her small breasts that sag like half moons at night. No, he said to the pastor, indicating with his hand the graves and their alignment toward the water, chalky and fitful below them. I'll show you what they were seeking. It is the sea. It is only—and that is everything—the sea.

The Faroese walks, directed by wind and scent. He slept that morning in one of Copenhagen's public parks, next to a monument that, like all Copenhagen's monuments, has been walled in against the bombs that have not come and will not come. The monument, finished in 1829, depicts one of Frederick VI's effete sons balanced precariously astride an armored horse. The son would have preferred a sculpture with one of his beloved clocks, of which he commissioned no fewer than sixteen hundred from the royal clockmaker and sent the united kingdoms of Denmark and Norway into a debt that only a war with Sweden could alleviate. But his father demanded a horse. After falling off a cart pony three times the prince posed straddling a low fence and the sculptor carved the horse from memory. Even then the sculptor's practiced fingers could not fully erase the look of surprise from the prince's face. The sculptor neglected to affix the prince's name to the statue and thus that has fallen into history. The Faroese slept last night warmed by the bricks surrounding the statue, the armored charger lurching forward, any moment, to crush him.

Now he walks down a treeless hill and, subtly, away from the light and into the voluntary ghetto. Jews mostly, but not exclusively: Gypsies, Turks, Czechs, Kazakhs, the wide range of damaged Europe. The air is thick with vernacular tongues. Smell bumps into smell like crowds at a boxing match. A game of backgammon between two Arab men on the sidewalk determines marriages of four future generations. They have come from Germany, many of them, but not only; Germany is not the only country that knows how to create refugees.

To the Faeroese the voluntary ghetto seems constructed entirely of glass; not literally, of course, because in fact hardly any glass exists anymore amongst the storefronts and what glass remains is covered with a thick grease to discourage rock-throwing. Instead he thinks of glass now because of an episode from his childhood. He lived with his mother and father in a sod house on a barren outcropping near a Faeroe Island town of little consequence. All of their belongings were distressingly simple. Only one glass decanter filled with whale oil stood out among an unending line of wooden cups and stone cookware. One day he arrived home to find that his two elder brothers had drowned; their boat capsized in a squall and they floated in to shore, two days later, empurpled and swollen. The boy watched as his mother lifted the glass decanter over her head. The whale oil soaked in golden window light and on the decanter's curved front two mermaids held each other in affection or fear. His mother said, Don't hold yourself anything precious in this world. It will only leave you. And with her left hand smashed the decanter against the table.

The Faeroese thinks of this—the temporality of all things—as he walks through the voluntary ghetto, but of course he cannot articulate that and so he imagines every single person in the ghetto packed into the glass decanter and soaked in whale oil. Under an awning he comes across two Jewish boys beating a third for his parents' egg money. He separates them by the shoulders. They run off, three together, to resume somewhere else. A Gypsy woman whose handkerchiefs and skirt and three scarves hang about her like air pushes to his nose a bag of spices that recalls pashas and sheiks and a 14th century massacre in Albania. He turns down a side street. He walks alone for several minutes, amidst hanging laundry and boarded windows. He encounters a beggar whose clothes seem stitched together from a dwarf's wardrobe. The beggar offers him the *memorbuch* of the Jewish community of Sulzbach, Bavaria, in

which are recorded 1,516 deaths, 724 births, twenty-three pogroms and two false messiahs. For a heel of bread he can add his name to the list. All of this is lost on the Faeroese because, as previously said, he cannot read. After handing him the book the beggar slumps against a doorway. After another moment he slips to the ground, asleep or dead, it is impossible to tell. The Faeroese puts the book under the beggar's head, leaves him there. Later, when the street cleaners come, the beggar will be hauled off and buried and the book will be cut up and pulped and remade into propaganda pamphlets and papers that fall from the sky.

The Faeroese sleeps that night in a doorway. When he thinks of food, a woman two stories above will throw down three slices of moldy bread. They taste to him just fine.

✠ ✠ ✠

And where does Bakman go now, Sunday afternoon, after the café? Back to the hospital. To the morgue. Not on the hospital's time, but on his own. He wants to play in someone else's body. He wants to plunge his arms elbow-deep in another person's abdomen. The parts, you see, are fluid, once past the stubborn barrier of the skin. Once inside anything can happen. Bakman plays to the audience spread on tables and opened drawers. Ladies and gentlemen, he says. And pulls intestines from an opened body like a handkerchief hidden in his sleeve. He stitches arteries into a pattern of lace. One time, practicing on a pair of indigent cadavers, he gave a man two livers, two stomachs, two hearts. Nobody knew the difference.

3

the edge of something greater

HANNAH'S FATHER IS A THIN man, bird-like in appearance. Wire-rimmed glasses sit low on his nose. He looks at his daughter through those glasses, blinking twice, as if expecting something to come into focus. Copenhagen businessmen have noticed how he uses those glasses as a tool, staring fiercely down through the lenses, or whipping them off in a grand gesture of outrage or surprise that rarely fails to lower the price of a purchase or increase the margin on a sale.

You want to do what? he says.

Come with you, Hannah says. Her father has arrived home from the paper mill in the middle of the day, washed, and put on his best suit, the one he wears only at holidays and weddings, so he can watch a Nazi parade through the middle of Copenhagen. He's clean-shaven, as always, and Hannah can see a neat line of close-cropped grey hair beneath the line of his bowler hat.

I don't know, he says. It'll be crowded. You might get . . .

I'll be fine, Hannah says. Look, she says, holding out a paper bag, which she opens for his inspection. It's filled with butter cookies. I made something to eat, she says.

Which was partially true. Actually she had stood in the kitchen while the maid pounded, creamed, mixed. The maid, a dull, round-faced woman, worked for several families in their comfortable Bellahøj neighborhood and seemed to have no preference in employers, Jewish or otherwise. Nor did she need much prodding to roll her sleeves past her elbows and make butter cookies, even with the makeshift materials available. It seemed that, given counter space and sufficient light, she could happily continue producing butter cookies even if the only baking ingredients left were chalk and puddlewater. While the maid baked Hannah read aloud from the society pages and announcements of the latest fashions of the Danish royal family.

The maid had left just after lunch and Hannah spent the early afternoon reading Sofie Østenmuller's letter from Palestine. It ran to so many pages that it seemed to have lengthened in the intervening years between its posting and its arrival. The letter gave an address—current as of 1939—of a group of young people in Copenhagen who planned to leave Denmark and emigrate to Palestine. Zionists, Sofie called them. It was a strange word, harsh at first and then sliding on long vowels toward a pleasant conclusion. Hannah tried it on in her bedroom, looking at herself in her hand mirror. I am a Zionist, she thought. Then turned the hand mirror to catch a profile of her thin face. There's Hannah Bergstrom, she thought. She's a Zionist.

Her mother was an obstacle, but not so serious a one as her father, which was why she felt bound to accompany him that afternoon to the parade. Her mother would miss her, of course, and worry, but her father—well, other things got in the way.

As they walk from Bellahøj to the center of Copenhagen, passing elegant houses and blooming gardens, her father explains why he has left the paper mill on a busy afternoon to view this parade. The parade's purpose, as reported in the papers, was to celebrate the installation of a new German governor in Denmark—the former governor having been packed off to Berlin after failing to properly address the growing cells of Communists, Socialists, and other political radicals who had recently developed such personality in Denmark, publishing shrieking newspapers, taking over radio broadcasts, and just that week, trying to blow up a train track near Copenhagen's Central Station.

We're an orderly country, her father says. We're not a bunch of criminals. He shook his head. From his tone it was clear he considered the protestors a half step above corner thugs, even Cohen, a Jew who signed his name to several editorials denouncing the relationship between Germany and Denmark. What's he trying to do to us? her father says, as they pass a shop displaying porcelain supperware and an ornate silver epergne. And she knows what else he thinks, because she's heard him say it: We've come so far. From a peddler ancestor. Only seventy years before, his own grandfather, pushing a heaping cart of worn clothing and cheap magazines through back alleys in this European city. To which he has found a key to the front doors, a key composed of business and money and correct behavior. It has been a long journey for him, ignoring slights and throwing dinner parties that fifteen years ago no one would attend, and now other Copenhagen businessmen, Jews and non-Jews, begged him for invitations and the chance to sip his brandy and praise his wife's newest evening dress.

And she would undo all that. Break open that journey like an eggshell and start over with the shattered pieces. Not here in Copenhagen, a solid, well-appointed city, but in a dusty, dry place where—according to Sofie's letter—the best item a person could possess was a working tractor. A place her father had described more than once as a barren country, half-wild with Arabs.

Her father stops at a kiosk and leafs through business papers in several languages before choosing one. He digs in his coat pocket for the right number of kroner, thumbs them onto the counter one at a time, then counts them again. He tucks the paper under his arm and they walk on.

✠ ✠ ✠

In the summer of the previous year he stumbled upon a crashed plane. He was trailing a group of wild sheep, their coats matted with feces, when he caught his toe on an slice of curled metal. This was at Slattaratindur, on the island of Eysturoy. It was the highest point in all the Faeroes. The ground where he fell was slick rock, interspersed with patches of damp, sickly-smelling moss. When he looked up he saw the plane.

It was a British plane, a Spitfire, a hunter of other planes, and sadly astray to find its way here. It stretched out propeller-first toward the tip of the mountain, as if it had been in the process of skimming up the side when its front end was crumpled by a wide, bulging rock. A blackened ring ran from behind the wings and cockpit clear to the tail, smudges and half-strokes of paint where numbers had been. The plane itself seemed to hold dissenting views about its own destruction. The left wing had clove clean off and sat as its own piece some ways down the mountain. The right wing hung fully attached to the fuselage, but it had shredded so that the entire armature of machine gun inside lay exposed.

He walked to the cockpit, which had cracked, allowing water to drain inside. He examined the pilot, who had withered into an odd arrangement of bone and uniform. Sitting there, he looked composed, free of panic, like a doll dressed up in army clothes and then handled into correct posture. Without the skin the uniform was grossly oversized. It hung loose around the bony wrists.

He looked to the other side of Slattaratindur, where a group of sheep grazed lazily on a wide plain. The far end of the plain held a small pool of rainwater and behind that stood a row of craggy rocks like witnesses. A pilot of extraordinary skill could conceivably have cleared the peak of Slattaratindur and made a harsh landing there on that leeward plain. This one had not succeeded.

He inspected the plane all around and tried to recreate the events that led to this wreck. He imagined this pilot falling away from his squadron in confusion, amidst a storm or perhaps a skirmish. Instruments spiraling senselessly, the pilot tapping them in an attempt to restore their attention. And all about the cockpit a whirling greyness, like the first moments of creation before the separation of water and sky.

He knew that his island suffered under two hundred days of annual fog, so it must have been a gift or moment of luck for the pilot to see the brief, mossy dollop of plain from the clouds. Or maybe he just saw the black tip of Slattaratindur and took it for what it actually signified: the edge of something greater.

That first day at the plane he pulled the pilot from the cockpit and stripped him of his clothes. He unbuttoned the jacket and the shirt and bones spilled out and dropped with a clatter to the rocks below. He gathered the belongings under his arm and carried them back to his cottage. In the next few days the boys and certain young men of his island appeared wearing various pieces of the pilot's uniform: cap, jacket, pants, a leather helmet. The boots he kept for his own use. It was as if a new style gripped the normally fashionless island for the length of that summer and the style could be described as Dead Englishman. Later he returned to the plane and stripped it of gears and other machine parts and bartered them for goods of similar value. A working section of carburetor passed hands for a whole chicken. Other parts he left strewn about his yard.

He left just enough of the plane to suggest its original outline. Enough so that he could lower himself into the cockpit and imagine himself the sinking pilot catching the sight of the open plain beyond Slattaratindur, the last vision of earth before the fire.

Hannah and her father watch as the sun shines pitilessly on the parade of German soldiers that threads its way toward Slotsholmen, blockading traffic, imposing itself upon the regular workings of the Copenhagen day. The Germans paraded often; it seemed to come as naturally to them as eating or taking an afternoon nap. But the crowds today exceeded all reasonable expectation—usually the Germans just marched in front of sparse onlookers and briefly interested passersby. Not today. Fear and fascination, her father says, adjusting his glasses. Then turns to take in the abundant scene.

He had chosen them a spot on Ved Stranden, overlooking a wide, calm canal and backgrounded by Slotsholmen, a series of brown, stately buildings set on its own small island here at the center of the city. Water lapped the rich, brick buildings on all sides and the entire mass of structures looked to Hannah as if they had risen from the sea whole and remarkably preserved. The bright sun radiates in the ruddy bricks and Hannah feels as if their warmth reddens her face, even here on the opposite side of the canal and surrounded by fellow parade-watchers. The tallest building is Børsen, the Copenhagen stock exchange, with ornate gables and a famous spire composed of four green dragons clutching the roof and wrapping their tails around each other in a tower aimed at the sky. It's an impressive sight,

Hannah thinks, though she wonders now as she had before why the architect chose to arrange these dragons with their asses pointed toward heaven.

The soldiers have been marching for several miles by the time they arrive at Slotsholmen, though when the first black-helmeted, grey-uniformed contingent passes by they seem to Hannah unaffected by the heat, the long walk, the heavy rifles. They just march. Only the small group of Danish Nazis walking behind the initial platoon seem worn by the parade and the exertion; they were a group of mostly fat middle-aged men in brown shirts that looked specially made for the occasion, outfitted in shining medals and Nazi armbands but with visible darkened sweat stains in the armpits and crotch. With a lift of his chin Hannah's father indicates among the Danish group a man who had been at their house for dinner before the war. Hannah and her father edge toward the front of the spectators to get a better view. Her father is polite but firm; he hasn't come all this way just to be crowded in the back. Hannah reaches in her bag—difficult work with the packed crowd—and takes out a pair of wrapped peaches. Despite her mother's precautions, several bruises darken their skin. She offers one to her father. When he bites it, sticky juice pools at the corners of his mouth.

She is very close now, as the fresh-shaven soldiers march by and the new German governor's car turns onto Ved Stranden, moving toward her. She stands on her toes to see him. He does not disappoint. He sits at perfect attention in the back of a shined black Mercedes. On his chest Hannah can see numerous medals. The swastika at his collar pinches his throat tight and he looks shorter than she expected, but he carries it off well. The grand car rolls by and the German seems impervious to the crowd, not waving or even looking but leaning forward just noticeably to give instructions to the driver. The car passes by and turns left on a short bridge into Slotsholmen itself, where it will stop in front of the Parliament building and the German will step out and be received with bows and handshakes by all the members of the Danish government.

Still more soldiers marching. Hannah's right in the front now, and she wants to leave, but her father has drifted back and she's caught on all sides by a group of young boys. One boy with sandy hair knocks the last peach out of her hand and it drops with a wet thud and another boy jostles her from behind. She shoves the first boy to create space and he falls abruptly out of the crowd and into the midst of the marching Germans.

The parade ripples, a quiver in the muscle. The soldiers have no training to account for this, a boy interrupting their parade. The thump-thump of the marching interrupted and now the German looking back to see what causes this disturbance. And the sandy-haired boy frozen in the street as a young German soldier, gawky and nineteen, pulls his rifle back to club him out of the way. And a dark-haired man in a ragged fishing sweater grabbing the Danish boy by the collar and yanking him back into his space in front of Hannah as the soldiers step forward and march on.

Hannah turns to see this man, but he's already moving backward into the crowd and away from her. On her right her father. She tugs once on his sleeve to indicate her departure, and follows.

She sees the man in the fishing sweater step backward out of the crowd, the space he occupied already filling with people like water into a tidal pool. He turns down an alley and begins to walk. Hannah follows him. As she follows she crosses a bridge over the Slotsholmen canal with him some distance in front of her and she's already moving away from the Copenhagen she knows. As she walks the bleating and stamping of the parade wanes distant and more distant and then mute. He's walking away from her. After turning left and left again and then right she sees a flash of black and thinks she has caught him but it turns out to be only a bed sheet hung over a doorway. She takes the sheet in her hand as if to pull it away and see what it covers but she thinks better of it and continues walking.

The streets run narrow and indistinct and the windows she passes small and unwelcoming and it is not like the Copenhagen of her childhood but some other Copenhagen more ancient and unwholesome. Some of the alleyways are so narrow she can press her palms flat against both walls at once and she has to duck under hanging shirts, bed linens, underwear. She loses sight of him for minutes at a time. She keeps walking. Then she sees him again, black hair and black fishing sweater, at the end of an alley. Once it seems to her that he looks over his shoulder to check on her progress. Entering the street market of the ghetto her hand brushes unknowingly against the apartment building where her mother conceived her with her father's help and which her father sold in April of 1940, the month the Germans arrived.

Despite the congested business of the street she can see him, taller and more upright than the vendors and street hawkers and moving lightly through the crowd. The street reeks of backed-up sewage and stale water. A lone violinist dressed in rags scrapes out an abbreviated melody. A woman in cabaret makeup offers her a tin of sweets that upon opening contains fish eyes. Hannah hands it back and follows the man in the fishing sweater.

This is not a place she would have come to before. Not before the war, not even two weeks ago. She has lived in Copenhagen her entire life and yet she cannot name this present neighborhood. It is near Christianshavn, that is all. And even Christianshavn is a place she wouldn't normally go, a poor neighborhood where her parents lived following their marriage and left as soon as her father acquired the mill and do not speak of now, not even laughing or with nostalgia. The workers of the paper mill still live here, she thinks, but how would she know?

And yet this Hannah is not even the same Hannah as before the war. That Hannah wanted vaguely to grow up and get married and certainly never to leave Denmark, especially for a place as uncertain and half-imagined as Palestine; that Hannah would not quit her professor in mid-lecture to stare at a grimy dock; and that Hannah would not follow a strange man into a dangerous neighborhood on a briefly-witnessed act of kindness. But she wants to speak with him. She has opened this organ of curiosity within herself, and it has taken on blood and oxygen like any other organ, and it is guiding her in the direction of a dark-haired man in an old fishing sweater. Who is now gone. Replaced by a beggar who approaches her, hand out, and she backs away.

I'm going to have a lot of explaining to do to my parents, she thinks, for the second time in as many days. By the time I get back from here, wherever it is, it'll be dark, and they'll be waiting. I'll have to explain all this at some point, and soon, she thinks. What will I say?

But as she turns the next corner he's waiting for her. He does not speak. She hears behind her the commotion of the market: footsteps, prices, the aching violin. His eyes like ash and his hair the color of squid's ink and again, that ratty sweater. He's looking at her. She follows him to a small recessed alleyway leading to a boarded-up door. Inside he has spread an old blanket, apparently on which to sleep. Next to it the remnants of food tins and waxed paper. The archway is narrow and to enter she must stand very close to him. Her throat is tight, asthmatic. She is near enough now to smell him and he smells like something out of her childhood. He has not stopped looking at her. Nor has he spoken. Hannah looks at him and there seem few options in this narrow shelter but she's a Zionist now so why not?—and slides her hand under his sweater and the worn cotton shirt beneath it and his muscles are as hard as fishing line. He doesn't move and so she reaches up to kiss him and when she does he tastes as cold and salty as the sea.

4

what he would acquire

Carl walked to his fishing boat in the failing dusk light down the small, curved streets of Gilleleje. A young boy tottered by him on shaky bicycle wheels. The wheels themselves were only bare rims and they clattered and threw sparks here and there against the street stones. The rubber owed to those wheels, Carl thought. He imagined a heavy troop carrier rumbling through a dismal forest bearing the martial flag of some country. Carl had patched and re-patched his own tires so many times since the war began that he didn't even bother to pull his bicycle from behind the house. He just walked. Two miles from his house through Gilleleje to the harbor. And in the morning, two miles back again.

Jette would leave tomorrow. His back ached as he walked and he passed a row of small houses in colors of washed peach and apricot. Others just white and all adorned on top with thick brown blankets of thatch. The streets were narrow and he could see in the windows of the houses he passed. He saw one old man leaning over a radio with his ear cocked to the face and tapping on the side as if to coax out sound or release a spirit. The next house had a patchy window box of flowers and within its small living room two children examined a thick book under a flickering gas lamp. The little girl was pretty and blond and reached to turn the pages of the book but her brother pushed her hand away. Behind them in the kitchen Carl saw a fellow fisherman in bib and overalls gathering food into his lunchbox. He was shod only in socks and he bent over the table. Next to him his tall rubber boots stood like attendants. Carl didn't wait for him and walked on.

And Jette. They had struck a compromise with the understanding that neither of them were at all satisfied. She would go to Copenhagen tomorrow. It's only overnight, but it will be the first time they've been apart in twenty-four years, save for the two nights Jette spent in the Helsingør hospital after her second miscarriage. Carl remembered the way she slept in the tiny hospital bed, the acrid smell of the hospital room, the way Jette twisted in the bed at night, so that her hospital gown would ride up nearly to her hip, and Carl would have to reach out to cover her bare legs or else turn his head away. He remembered also the grey-haired, abrupt nurse who came in the room at all hours to inject Jette with various solutions, this to make her sleep, that to adjust her fluids, as if anything in those tiny syringes could make up for everything she had lost there. He remembered those needles, so tiny and metallic, like the numbers on each of the houses he passes, some stamped iron, others just daubed in paint. Each of the houses carried a set of numbers to mark it, a simple house number and also the date that the house was built. Most of the houses were over a hundred and fifty years old. The families maintained the numbers on their houses, no matter how small the dwellings, as if to make themselves more permanent on earth by their houses' own stubborn survival.

Tomorrow Jette would go. The doings in their house were meager and would not suffer too greatly in her absence. But what about him? Carl knew that she would prepare three meals for the time she'd be gone, a spread of cheese and pork for lunch, boiled potatoes and fish for dinner, and leave directions for preparing his breakfast porridge in her cramped, delicate handwriting. The food would taste good, and he would feel an immense sadness at each meal.

He passed a pub with few customers. The bartender had set out a small *koldtbord* of bread and salted fish, but the drinkers at the bar mostly ignored it and attended to their beers. A dog sat outside the pub door. It pricked up one ear as Carl passed and then returned to its previous state of minimal activity.

He felt his back pinch as he turned to the north and the harbor peeked into view between two small warehouses. Fishing boats lined the docks. The water was calm and the boats only strained slightly against their moorings. Carl saw his own boat, the *Jette*, blue-hulled like the rest of the Gilleleje boats, which enabled the fisherman to distinguish themselves from those of Tisvildeleje to the west and Hornbæk to the south. The *Jette* was only as long as a car and the width of a breakfast table at its widest point. It featured a cabin at the back end, an upright rectangle that resembled most closely an outhouse, barely tall enough for a man to stand in. In that way, it had little to distinguish it from the twenty or so fishing boats that crowded the dock.

Most of the other fishermen had already arrived. They sat in a circle at the close end of the dock, their feet toward the center as if to warm them at some imaginary fire. They sat on their lunchboxes and some on posts and moorings. They were a solid-looking group of men and Carl had known almost all of them for twenty years. He had had at least one conflict with each of the men over that time, questions of territory and fish, but the conflicts had resolved reasonably in time and he held no particular grudges. The men sat with their thermoses open, the cup ends steaming in the late afternoon light. Carl distrusted groups but to shun them would be obvious. Instead he placed his satchel to the left of the circle and sat against an open dock pillar. His back cramped against the pressure of the wood and he shifted into a half-sitting, half-crouched position, using his hand on the side away from the group to steady himself.

Get on with it, Carl heard a man say. It was Poul Andersen, one of the younger of the group. Carl had fished with his father in the 1930's. He was talking to Martin Borch, a man about Carl's age. We're losing light, the man added. Carl turned to the Sound and saw that the sky had reached a brilliant blue, the way the world falls into sharper focus as the day ends.

I'll get right to the point, Martin said. Martin had grown fat in the middle in the last few years and he had a habit of rubbing his stomach as he talked. A fishing boat sank last night, he said.

Carl counted the circle of fishermen. None were missing. This was in Tisvildeleje, Martin said.

What happened? said Anders Mortensen. Who Carl had seen partially dressed in his kitchen. Carl felt a sudden bloom of shame spread against his chest when he remembered that intimacy. He looked at Martin.

The man's name was Peter Hansen, Martin said. He was trolling out in the Kattegat when he hit something sharp. His boat cracked in half and fell out underneath him. Another fisherman nearby heard the sound—it was a terrible sound, the man said, like thunder breaking in the water—and he saw a black shape sinking into the water.

A U-Boat? Anders Mortensen asked.

That's right. The other fishing boat motored over there, trailing his nets, but Hansen was already gone. What was strange, Martin added, was how little of Hansen's boat was left, just a few jagged boards.

Carl smelled the odors of the harbor, the wet rope, the stink of fish coming off the dock under his boots. Men stood up. Martin turned over his hat to collect for the fisherman's widow. A couple of men stepped forward and dropped in a few coins. Others did not. Like Carl, they carried no money, afraid their wives would lose those few kroner along with everything else if they went down at sea.

Some left the circle to untangle their nets or check small matters on their boats. Martin sat with his fat haunches on his lunchbox. Right to the bottom, he said. Carl watched Martin mimic the U-boat's descent into the water, angling his hand in a sharp motion from his left shoulder to his right hip. Right to the bottom, he said again, and Carl hated him.

Poul Andersen had begun to walk to his boat at the far end of the dock. He had a young wife, only seventeen, and two weeks ago this wisp of a wife had brought their new son to the fisherman's church for the first time. When Carl had seen the baby a terrible thought had flashed into his head: if you drop that baby right now, it'll break its head open like a melon on the church floor. It'll be dead before anybody can move.

Poul Andersen stopped on the way to his boat and said to Martin, Why did you tell us this? So we can turn around and go home? Isn't one of us can do that, he said. Martin just shrugged. Then he rose from the lunchbox and set off for his boat, the *Anna*, named for his mother.

Anders Mortensen nodded at Carl as he passed and asked him where he expected fish that day. Carl told him of a spot far into the Sound, near the rocky shoreline of Sweden, but didn't mention his second spot to the east, along the old Oslo-Stockholm ferry route, now abandoned because of the war and little used.

The others pushed off before him because Carl was slowed by his back and by a faint desire to prolong this aspect of his day. He waited while other fishermen rumbled into the Sound and the *Jette* sat solitary at the dock, a lone tooth in a worn mouth. By trailing the others he might also avoid inspection by a German patrol boat. Every few nights he encountered one of the sleek, powerful boats with the garish broken cross painted on its sides. Its searchlight would flutter over him in the dark, an obscene firefly, and he would cut his motor and wait while a German officer marked down on a clipboard the status of his catch, the number, the type, the time of night, and his exact position on the water. While on the patrol boat a low-rank and sullen soldier would stand, a single-bolt rifle pointed at Carl, as if Carl, alone in the water, might start some one-man rebellion against the Third Reich. It was humiliating.

He took an extra moment to clear his netting and to set his coffee thermos and dried mutton under his seat, even though these things could be accomplished as he motored out into the water. He breathed in the stink of the fishhouses behind him mixed with the salt water. Carl had never been reluctant toward the sea and had no more than a healthy fear of it but in the last few years he entered it more slowly, like an older lover pausing to admire a woman's body before touching her skin.

As he turned the key the boat hiccupped to life and Carl scanned the water in front as he moved from the dock. Nothing. If he had noticed one thing about the Germans it was their desire for recordkeeping. They seemed to want to make their mark on the world through efficient administration. It was as if all the penetrations of neighboring countries were simply a way for them to show how they could handle the affairs of each place so much better than the indigenous population.

As he edged into the Sound, placid in the early evening, he found himself scanning for a pattern in the water, a reflection off glass that might suggest a periscope. Conversation at the docks was filled with odd and grotesque ways that fishing boats might wreck; in that way, Carl figured, they were scarce removed from the days of the Kraken and other mythical sea creatures. Still, a U-Boat marked a new entry in the realm of fishing boat disaster, a list already plenty long, Carl thought: dead motor, rocks, fog, storm, leak, drowning. It was not lost on Carl that the Tisvildeleje fisherman had died simply due to the U-Boat's existence and the random allocation of positions on the water. There was only so much space. It would be easier to take if the U-Boat had fired on the fishing skiff. At least the man would be intentionally dead and his wife would have some particular being to hate. But no. The fishing skiff had just happened upon the U-Boat like some enormous evolved whale. I'm not losing you to an accident, Jette said to Carl one night while they ate dinner. That's the only way you'll lose me, Carl smiled back at her. But when he reached for her hand she moved it away.

Shortly after midnight Carl looked at his half-load of fish and knew that he would not reach a full load that night. He had chewed the mutton and drank most of the coffee and twice interrupted his work to piss over the side of the boat. His catches seemed lower each year. Now, since the Germans arrived, prices had slipped as well. The Germans bought nearly all the fish; they set the prices. Not unfair prices, not cheating prices. But low prices.

And even if there were enough fish, and the money arrived, what would you buy? Carl thought of himself as a man who didn't need much in the way of objects, but he did notice that the three long years since the occupation began had placed a strain upon himself and Jette. It was a slow squeezing, but he didn't think it could be escaped in Copenhagen or anywhere else in the narrow realm of places he'd been.

The water thumped against the side of the boat. His back throbbed worse at night, and he wanted a cigarette. It had been a pleasant routine for him, smoking while he fished, something to keep the mouth and hands occupied during the many lonely hours. But he had given it up. This was two and a half years ago, when German patrol boats had first appeared in the Sound. He could see, even then, that life under the Germans would become a series of trading scarce goods for other scarce goods. In his mind he had constructed a type of schematic—what he would acquire, even at raised prices: milk, coffee, wood, other materials to keep their house repaired. And what he would not: tobacco, new clothes, anything that he considered a gift. He had done this, but it had never sat easily with him. And now he was in a world in which a man could not sail out to fish and reasonably expect to come back alive.

I do not wish it, he had said to the pastor.

Tomorrow Jette would leave for Copenhagen to visit her sister. The sister worked as a seamstress in a small third-floor shop, a hot and noisy whir of sewing machines. Her husband repaired car engines. The two of them lived in Christianshavn, a working-class neighborhood where drinking seemed the main occupation. But Jette. She noticed things. What do you do there? he had asked her, regarding her visits to Copenhagen. I just look, she said, as if it were an activity requiring no further explanation.

I do not wish it, he had said.

He leaned forward in the boat and felt the inside of the planking where he knew a board was cracked. Cool and dry. It would hold for now. He had moved once, when he was seventeen, and had found the experience so uprooting and baleful he had no desire to repeat it. First, the girl in the barn. Then the wandering from Fyn, his home, to Lolland, to Falster, to Møn, endless fields of sugar beets that ran right up to the water. Then to Gilleleje. He had walked across Sjælland at a heading directly north, a direction chosen only because it demanded little adjustment of his hand-held compass. He had stopped at the beach in Gilleleje, the northernmost point in Sjælland, though at the time he thought he might just keep walking into the water. Instead he turned around. He got work in the fishhouses at the dock, met the slight, pretty Jette, married her. Took over her father's boat. Now he's one of the Gilleleje fishermen, who he can't see but knows are out there, dotting the Sound. After twenty-five years these men think of him, though with perhaps only one section of their four-chambered hearts, as one of them. It has taken this long. Carl no longer let Jette see his catches, how small they were. He didn't tell Jette that when he walked to the dock in the morning he saw that nearly all the men were his age, that there were no young men to replace them, that if they moved to Copenhagen it would be as poor and penniless as orphans.

He cranked the motor and moved to his second spot. After an hour he finished the coffee. Against the black sky he saw clouds the color of smoke spreading from end to end. He took off his hat to face them bareheaded. He was deep into the Sound now, into the black water. The sea smelled rich and hungry. If that plank sprung a leak now, if the tar holding it melted or if he caught his sweater in the net and got pulled over the sea would swallow him and his body would not return to the shore. He would disappear. Or the tide would carry his body, whitened and nicked with fish bites, to Sweden or to Norway and he would disappear that way. The warring parties would not stop to return him. He would vanish. It would be easy. He looked over the side of the boat at the rolling water an arm's length below him. The salt water lapped against the side of the boat. It called to him. It would be easy.

Bakman is sure he would sleep better if not for the monkeys' screeching. He looks at his pocket watch, the one with the Roman numerals and exposed casing. Three o'clock. In the morning. The screeching might last anywhere from twenty minutes to three hours. Emanating from the Copenhagen Zoo, just down the street from Bakman's boardinghouse, it bellows up through the window, metal scraping against metal or the hands of a watch rolling backwards. You you you, the monkeys screech, Get away. You you get away. Bakman cannot be sure that's what they screech, of course, but he thinks that's it because when he wakes up sweating in the middle of the night that's what he wants to scream.

The pretty nurse is in his bed, awake. Her name is Marina. Bakman has crossed to the window, which is open to better accommodate the monkeys' screeching. Marina smokes a cigarette. That looks awkward, Bakman thinks. The whole of Copenhagen squats under a German-ordered blackout and the cigarette hanging from her lips provides the only illumination, it seems to Bakman, in the entire Nørrebro neighborhood. Its orange tip, glowing when she inhales, casts a faint light on her naked upper torso, pooling in the crevice between her neck and her collarbone. She's sitting upright in the bed while she smokes and the blanket lingers at her waist not because she wishes to be daring or to excite Bakman again but because to cover herself seems like too much trouble.

Bakman knows he didn't do a very good job during sex. It wouldn't bother him so much but he's sure Marina has also slept with his friend Henrik, who happens to live in the room next to Bakman. Henrik reads the resistance newspaper *Frit Danmark* and claims to have smuggled medical supplies to the growing partisan movement in Fyn and Langeland. If asked to operate on a German soldier Henrik claims he will refuse. Either that or drop a Danish krone into the German's bile duct and give him something to remember Denmark by. Why don't you sew in a signed picture of Christian X while you're at it? Bakman said. Maybe I will, Henrik replied. Maybe I will.

It was Henrik who convinced Bakman to hire that Jewish cleaning woman, even though she speaks no Danish and the few German words Bakman knows just drop at her feet like unopened letters. Another of Henrik's ridiculous gestures, taking on a German refugee as a cleaning woman even though the woman had no aptitude whatsoever for cleaning. Bakman tried every week to direct her indifferent scrubbing but all his efforts came to nothing.

What are they going on like that about? Marina says. Bakman knows that once she leaves this room he'll never see her naked again and so he's wondering if he should try another go with her. She reminds him of a girl you'd see walking along some farm road in the countryside: dirty blond hair, complacent eyes. He half wonders if she's left her milk pail in some corner of his room.

The moon, Bakman says. The moon always gets them worked up. But the moon is just a pale sliver tonight, like a finger tracing a bowl's edge, and so if the monkeys are screeching it's not at the moon itself they howl but rather at its absence.

Stepping back now, laying over this moment a scene from say, the 1936 Danish film *The Painter* or a similar German Expressionist effort, something from before the Nazis changed them all into propaganda films, what would we see? The distance between Bakman and Marina; the meager room and its bare furniture; the theme of orange cigarette light—transferred somehow into black and white celluloid—carried from bed to table to window and past Bakman and down to the zoo below the flat where it is picked up in the fur of the tiger. It is a Bengal tiger, Bakman thinks; he read that once while walking in the zoo. Trapped or drugged in its richly hued equatorial home only to awaken here. Bakman has watched the tiger pace the fourteen-foot length of its cage. The large cat covered it in three steps. In Indonesia the tiger's coat hides it seamlessly in the vegetation; here it is revealed by every stone sidewalk and grey storefront. Bakman has watched a German soldier—an eighteen-year-old with fuzzy ears on patrol in the zoo—carefully line up that tiger in his rifle sight, load a shell, and snap home the hammer. And smile.

✠ ✠ ✠

The bellowing of a boat horn roused him. Carl jerked up to see a large ferryboat cutting through the water toward his skiff. Backed by the clouds and the nighttime darkness the ship seemed to emerge directly out of Carl's memory. A sight from before the war. The phrase caught him and he stood straight. *Before the war.* He hadn't seen a ship like this in over four years: a vacation boat, carrying travelers on the Norway-to-Sweden run. As it moved closer he recognized the ship itself, the *Vestfjord,* out of Oslo. He had seen it many times, but not here, not at this section of the Sound. Carl remembered how the Norwegian and Swedish passengers would sun themselves on the deck as they passed—men in their shirtsleeves and women bearing wide hats to protect their fair skin. He would see a young couple standing together against the rail and sometimes Carl would even raise his hand to wave.

But a ship at this heading, this far south, would not have Sweden as its destination. It would be heading to Germany, probably to Stettin or Danzig on the North Coast. Carl performed these calculations effortlessly, instantly; he had performed them his entire adult life and did them without thinking.

The boat took a heading close to Carl. He didn't have time to pull his nets. The ferry would have to adjust course, if it even saw him. If not, it would charge right over him and crush the *Jette* like a walnut shell.

Carl looked over his left shoulder and tried to discern the shores of Gilleleje. It was so far he couldn't see it. If he jumped now he would avoid the ferry but likely be swamped in the wake. He could get crushed by the wreckage of his own boat. In any case it was a long swim, even for a young man. Which Carl was not. He reached into the cabin and tugged on his horn two full blasts. They carried forth from his boat like low-octave birds. He saw the wake of the *Vestfjord* peel away slightly.

The *Vestfjord* drew close and the *Jette* began to rock in anticipation. The blue hull of the ferry approached like a whale and it sat low in the water with its fullness. When he looked up he saw a deck crammed full with passengers, all dressed in their best clothes, men in suits and hats, women in long dresses, all staring straight ahead as if trapped at some humorless dinner party. Their luggage piled next to them and falling over at each lurch of the ferry. Some of the men bent to pick up the luggage but others just left it sprawled against the deck, pushing against their ankles and the ankles of their wives. Two German soldiers leaned against the railing, their rifles slung carelessly by the strap over their shoulders, and when the ship passed right next to Carl's skiff one of the soldiers leaned over and spat into the water. Other soldiers stood among the crowd like idle waiters, distinguished only by their grey uniforms and conical black helmets. Carl looked down and saw a young girl's face framed by a porthole. He began to wave to her but his hand felt heavy and the girl's face, caught in the porthole, passed him by.

As the ferry motored by him the soldier who spat leaned over and looked at Carl. He was as close as a man leaning out his window to address his neighbor. He had a handsome face and a thin scar or pox mark on his jaw. When he passed directly over Carl he tilted his head to indicate his passengers and said: *Juden.* Then he pulled his right hand across his throat in a casual slashing motion. He did it as carelessly as scratching an itch. The other soldier laughed.

After the ferry delivering the Jews to Germany had shuffled down the Sound, Carl reined in his nets. Three fish. He drank the last swig of his cold coffee and cranked the skiff toward shore. Then he bent into his tiny cabin to retrieve his last stash of tobacco from under the wooden instrument panel. He had wrapped it in wax paper but when he tapped it into his rolling sheet it proved as damp as newspaper. He waved his fingers over it carefully as if to dry it and finally twirled it into a modicum of a cigarette. Still, he had trouble lighting it, though perhaps that was because his hands were shaking.

Forty-five minutes passed before he alighted, the first of the fishing boats to return. He packed his boat in the dark and dropped three fish into his haversack. He left the *Jette* and walked the twenty minutes home, arriving while it was still dark.

Carl took his boots off at the kitchen table. In the bedroom Jette slept as if she had been lowered full-bodied into a dream. One pink heel poked out from under the cotton night sheet. Next to the bed sat the floral suitcase she would take to Copenhagen. Carl left her there.

She finally woke an hour after her usual custom, with the morning light slanting over her entire side of the bed. She moved stumbling into the dining room disoriented, as if she had not quite worn away the curtain between the sleeping and the living. Carl did not encourage her. Finally she turned to the stove and began preparing breakfast.

They ate in silence. She cleared the plates and Carl took his boots outside to clean them. Afterwards, in bed, Carl's back aches as Jette rocks on top of him, rocking from the hips as he steadies her with his hands, and he pulls out of her before he comes so that there will be no pregnancy, even though it isn't enough time for her, even as it reminds him of yet another way in which they have become compromised.

1933

The ceaseless clicking of watch crystals. Bakman at fourteen. Banded light through the wide front window but it doesn't reach his father, white-haired and precise in his movements, bent over his workbench at the back of the shop. With a measured angling of the hand his father presses on a gear too tiny to see; one can only imagine its presence inside the watch itself, form in the mind the linkage of teeth and gears, then picture the link broken. Where would it be? His father's hands, brown with spots, unsteady until the moment the needle enters the watch backing, never probing, always aimed directly for this point or that point. Which spring loosened? Which mechanism to recurl? To set the contiguous motion aright and all the events thrust inevitably into sequence?

After four hours his father looks up, removes the magnifier that bloats his right eye, blinks at Bakman as if seeing him for the first time and says, Why aren't you in school?

School's out for the summer.

Is it that time already?

For two weeks now.

His father nods once, takes out his handkerchief, clears his throat, and spits horribly into the cloth. He inspects it for a moment, then folds the handkerchief and places it back in his pocket. Then he pulls the magnifier down over his eye and reenters the watch.

After another hour his father places the watch down on the bench, reaches down into his satchel and takes out a lunch wrapped in wax paper. He gives half to Bakman. Without leaving his chair he clicks on a radio, listens for the duration of the sandwich and turns it off the moment the last bite enters his mouth. The radio announces that unemployment in Scandinavia has risen to 41%, 43% in Denmark specifically. Election news in Germany. A royal wedding in England described.

Bakman crosses the distance between himself and the workbench. Parts lay strewn across the tabletop, devoid of sense. His father smells of goose liver and cigarettes. The boy leans over, peering into the opening above which the needle stands poised to enter. The boy's knee bumps the table. All the parts scatter. His father grabs him like a sprung trap. Without looking up, he says, Don't you ever do that again. The grip does not relax. His left hand holds Bakman just above the elbow and Bakman realizes that he could pull against that grip for the next hour and not come loose. After a long moment his father releases him. The boy returns to his chair. A half-hour passes and his father puts down the needle. He reaches into the satchel at his feet and pulls out a tarnished pocket watch. He wipes it once against his pants and holds it out for Bakman to take.

You want to play with something, play with this, his father says.

Is it valuable?

If it was valuable I'd sell it, he says.

Bakman rubs it with his shirtsleeve. Roman numerals on the face, the time correct. A plain backing that refuses to click closed. Bakman studies the mechanism but sees no relationship. Perhaps in time.

Bakman looks at the shop. Outside the window a bare street, little foot traffic. His mother already dead from cholera and his father to follow in two weeks. He looks at the watches suspended in their cases. Unclaimed. The repair bills unpaid. The crystals clicking ceaselessly. The needle poised above the opening.

6

all bodies equal

IT WAS THREE DAYS SINCE the parade, Christianshavn, the man in the fisherman's sweater. In that time she read Sofie Østenmuller's letter again and again, turning it in the light as if it contained secrets beyond the mere sentences. She pulled the laced sheets to her chest and settled into her bed, a high, puffy affair decorated with pleats and topped by a complicated system of bedding and pillows. At the base sat a white trunk painted lightly with pale flowers. All around her the room arranged with an eye toward excess. Hannah read slowly as Sofie described her long days working on her kibbutz, a small, unsure settlement in the Hula Valley. Of digging rows for tomatoes in ground still wet with swamp dirt. Then, at night, serving her rotation in the dining room as all were obliged to do, regardless of status, age, or gender. Washing dishes next to men, her sleeves rolled to her elbows and soap water clinging to her wrists.

You would not recognize me, she wrote. At times I do not even recognize myself.

Hannah heard her father's heavy steps enter the hallway. A door creaked, and a moment later she heard him pissing. It didn't last long. He jingled a chain and the toilet responded with water.

The door creaked again and Hannah heard him take two steps, pause, and step again, this time toward her room. She found herself folding Sofie's letter twice along its crease and tucking it under her arm.

Her father tapped lightly on her door, hardly a tap even. More like a brushing of the knuckles. Hannah? he said. Are you still awake?

Just reading, she answered. Everything's okay.

It's late, he said. Do you need anything? Should I wake your mother?

No, Daddy, she said. Go to sleep. I'll see you in the morning.

Okay, he said. Come get me if you need anything. Then he padded away. She unfolded the letter and returned to Sofie's narrative, which continued along the theme of transformation and discovery.

Sofie wrote in a long and intricate hand, a handwriting that struck Hannah as at odds with the scene that it described, though it brought such apparent longing from Hannah as she read it. She felt that she and Sofie should do no less than swap places, since her own room and writing desk and fine pens seemed to be the origin of the handwriting on the page, and she, the person receiving it, the one whose demeanor and callousness belonged in the mean tents of Palestine. Witness her shrugging off of her father just moments before. But they were not swapped. She was in floral, occupied Copenhagen and Sofie in a dirt field, where she described in one sentence the life cycle of a pepper plant, and in another, the equally fascinating shape of a young man from Romania, shirtless and sweating, smiling at Sofie from the next row of vegetables with a mouth only half-full with teeth.

At one point the letter stopped abruptly. A white space continued some way down the paper and then it began again. I do not even know why I'm writing this to you, Sofie said. Maybe just to spend a few hours in my own language. Her father and mother had moved down to Jaffa, she explained, where her father had found a job adjudicating land claims among newly arrived Jews. It suited his legal background, and anyway, he was a poor farmer. It meant, though, that Sofie had no one to speak with in Danish, and had to get by like all the other immigrants, struggling to identify even the simplest objects in her kindergarten Hebrew.

The problem of a new language. It hadn't even occurred to Hannah. In school she had studied Swedish for its practicality and proximity, Italian for its literature. But she had never gotten further in the *Inferno* than the areas reserved for minor sins, never mind the entire realms of the damned. She looked at her Dante on her bookshelf, side-by-side pages in Danish and Italian, all of it untouched for several years. As for Hebrew, well—she could count with two hands the entire extent of words she could match with their meanings. I have a great deal of work to do, she thought. She folded the letter and tucked it under the mattress. She pulled the covers to her chest again and fell asleep hoping to be visited by the man in the fisherman's sweater, or, at the very least, a young Romanian.

✣ ✣ ✣

For a few days he retains the smell of her in his tiny room. He keeps the window closed to trap it—a pungent, sexual scent mixed with the sweet odor of perfume—even though with the window shut a stifling heat gathers in the sheets, in the bathroom, in the medical books scattered angrily across the desktop. Also with the windows closed the monkey screeches do not penetrate the apartment with such impunity.

The pretty nurse was not so pretty as he had thought. Bakman realized that now. Her teeth were uneven and her skin pitted. She had round, soft breasts—Bakman remembered holding both of them in his hands—but her eyes were sullen and removed. Bakman felt his stomach grumble and moved to the kitchen—that is, to the kitchen section of the room—to negotiate some breakfast from the cupboard. He found a tin of butter and the heel of a black bread. Upon closer inspection the bread heel revealed a cluster of mold. He removed the spot with his thumbnail, but when he turned the bread over he saw that the mold had marched straight through to the other side, set up spotted little camps as was the way of its species. He could not eat it, nor bring himself to discard it. He put it down on the counter.

Eight a.m. Four hours until shift. Bakman opened the window to hear the planes circling overhead. He saw a two-propeller bomber with British markings and after six minutes a German one appeared to take its place. Another paper bombing. Bakman imagined himself as a crewmember in the German plane, wearing a leather jacket and goggles, hunched over the bombsight. We've spotted the enemy! A newspaper vendor! Open the doors! And the leaflets flutter from the belly like feathers, some flying back into the plane, one sticking to the side of Bakman's flight helmet, others floating down to bury the newspaper seller in a pile of SIEG HEILS.

Bakman the bombardier circled the apartment twice more, showering first the harbor and then the financial district with leaflets. As he flew over Copenhagen the leaflets changed, moving from a paean to the *Führer* to an instructional pamphlet on dental hygiene. The Germans might be on to something here, he thought. Imagine a new set of directions descending from the heavens every twenty minutes or so. TURN LEFT AT THE NEXT STREET. BUY A PIECE OF CHOCOLATE. Individual decision-making removed. Airborne morality. Henrik's the philosopher-king, Bakman thought. Let's see what he thinks of this phrase: *Airborne morality.*

Bakman's stomach called to him again. He tossed the moldy bread into the trash and decided to take his breakfast on the street. But where? He hadn't returned to the coffeehouse in Nyhaven in weeks. Bakman abhorred the idea of starting over. Of finding a new café, familiarizing himself once again with the menu, the tables, the arrangement of light. But as the café owner became more friendly,

Bakman grew uneasy. Society creates certain distances, Bakman thought, pulling on the black wool sweater he had worn since his university days. A hole had opened in the left armpit and Bakman had to proceed carefully, holding the sweater's sleeve with his right hand so he wouldn't tear the opening further. These distances keep us safe from one another. They keep us whole. Especially true in medicine. Henrik, with all his resistance talk, didn't understand that. What had Professor Bøge said? *All bodies equal under the knife.* Bakman remembered the professor's nicotine-stained fingers, the triangular beard that dominated the front of the Medical Ethics class. *Why do you think we put the gas mask on them? To anesthetize? No—to remove the face.* And then another lecture, from Death and Dying: *The dead ask for nothing—not even to be buried. Only the living ask for that.*

Bakman heard a commotion in the hallway, Henrik's door opening, a clunk on the floor. Then conversation. Bakman belatedly remembered that today was cleaning day. He cracked open the door and peeked into the hallway, all the while lifting up his sweater to tuck in his shirt. He saw Henrik's wide, beneficent face, his topping of straw hair, and next to him, coming only to the height of his breastbone, the Jewish cleaning woman. Henrik was telling her a story that seemed to involve his youth as a football goalie. Bakman had come to suspect that the cleaning woman was not from Germany, as Henrik claimed, but from Poland. Under the hesitant German she spoke to Henrik, Bakman heard wide Polish vowels and sloppy consonants. Like a man slipping across ice.

Bakman!

Bakman opened the door wider and took a step into the hallway. What? he said.

Stop skulking there and join the conversation. Look at you. Did you sleep in your clothes? A doctor must portray confidence, Bakman. You look like you spent the night rummaging with cats in the alleyway.

Bakman hastily finished tucking in his shirt. My shift doesn't start for four hours, he grumbled.

Then you better start getting ready now. Mine on the other hand, begins in ten minutes. So I'm off. I was just telling Mrs. Krebnow here about the all-Copenhagen finals in '36. Maybe you could finish the story for me. By the way, did you know she used to be the principal of a high school?

No.

No? You should take more time to get to know people.

She's a cleaning woman, Bakman replied.

Ah, Bakman, Henrik said. He started for the stairs. By the way, he said as he passed, I have to cancel our dinner plans for tonight. More of that business I mentioned to you. He winked at Bakman and disappeared into the stairwell while launching into an exaggerated rendition of *There is a Lovely Country.*

Bakman found himself staring dumbly at Mrs. Krebnow. Henrik and his resistance adventures. In ten years it'll be just another story he tells at cocktail parties. While some of us will have devoted our lives to serious medicine. The buzzing of a plane overhead vibrated briefly through the walls of the building. Mrs. Krebnow didn't seem to notice. She picked up her bucket of cleaning supplies and stood there in her shapeless smock, her grey hair pulled into a bun, waiting for Bakman to move from the doorway of his apartment. Why do we tolerate this woman? Bakman thought. If he could speak to her he would fire her. Go back to Warsaw, he wanted to say. Or Krakow, or wherever. He wanted to tell her that generosity has its limits, that even the Danish don't have boundless capacity for charity, that she needed to stop showing up in this hallway every other Wednesday. Did she think he had a fat wallet and money to spare? At the very least she should clean the bathroom properly. But instead he stepped from the entranceway and even held the door open for her as she shuffled by.

When he finally left the apartment he discovered that the paper bombing had been completed, but apparently a printing error had occurred, because all the leaflets had smeared completely black and carried no instructions at all.

Hannah came downstairs in the morning to find her parents already at breakfast, an arrangement of bread and jam on the table and their cups still half-filled with a dark tea. Her father was dressed in a brown suit and he had trimmed his mustache since the previous day and now sat carefully shaping his hat with a wooden block. He smiled at Hannah when she entered and then returned to the business of the hat, pinching the crown with thumb and forefinger and then holding it at arm's length for inspection and finally brushing it free of some particle or dust with the back of his other hand.

Hannah sat with them at the small wooden table adjacent to the kitchen, intended for breakfast and afternoon coffee but which they used for nearly all meals. There was an elegant table with great curved legs in the dining room and it reached nearly eight feet in length and in the early years of the occupation they had used it for Friday night and for Bergstrom's business dinners but in the last year they had set it only for holidays, if then. Last night they had taken Shabbos dinner at this small table with only a short *Kiddush* and *hamotzi* over two dinner rolls to mark the occasion.

As Hannah began to assemble a small breakfast her father stood up and announced that he had to take some meetings in Copenhagen. Don't expect me until the late afternoon, he said. He placed the hat on the crown of his head with care and smoothed the lapels of his suit. How do I look? he said, turning first to Hannah and then her mother. Very handsome, Hannah said, nodding. What more can I ask? he said, and looked at his two women with obvious pleasure. Then he left the house.

Hannah ate her breakfast, at the end daubing the crumbs with her finger and bringing them to her mouth. Her mother looked out the window, first at Bergstrom in his brown suit walking from the house and then at the space he had occupied. She turned to Hannah and smiled wanly.

Hannah's mother was a woman of admirable prettiness, the opposite of her daughter in many ways, small where Hannah was tall, graceful where Hannah was awkward. She had met Bergstrom at a family holiday dinner, found that he was a distant cousin. That fact made the marriage easy to arrange. He was only a university student then, one of the few she knew since that position did not open regularly to Jews, and did not expect to live beyond the income of their parents. When Bergstrom moved into business and became a success, she took it as good fortune rather than as necessity. She had given birth to Hannah ten months after her marriage and then two years later a son, who died mere days after his *bris.* She was prone to daydreaming, and didn't seek her daughter's company often.

Thus, it was a surprise when her mother turned to her and said, So, what shall we do today?

Why don't we go to the synagogue, Hannah found herself saying.

She didn't know why she had said that. She didn't want to go to the synagogue, a haughty top hat of a building just a few blocks from the university. Just the proximity to the university might make her blurt out some awkward confession about not going to her classes.

That's a quaint idea.

Her mother seemed unbalanced by the outrageousness of Hannah's request. But brightened at the thought of a walk in the city.

Her mother chose a high, bell-shaped hat of dated vintage for the outing. Along the way they paused often to inspect the windows of shops in the Latin Quarter. To Hannah it seemed strange that some store windows hung impossibly full with goods and fashions while others bore the full burden of the war's scarcities. Her mother commented that it simply reinforced that certain people had the ability to survive, no matter what the circumstances. Your father is one of those, she said, turning from a window.

Once at the synagogue they climbed the steps to the women's section and sat in the balcony, looking down at the men. The men prayed in rows and rows of high-backed pews that bore every similarity to the ledgers of her father's accounting books. At the front the rabbi led the service in a high church style, with much elaborate singing, and Hannah struggled to match this cantorial rendition of Hebrew with the clipped phrases Sofie described using on the kibbutz. To Hannah it seemed foolish that anybody would consider this stiff, ritualized language fit for daily use. It seemed just as unlikely that her mother would peel off their flowered wallpaper in long pasty strands and serve it as that night's dinner.

Hannah watched the men bow and quiver at the proscribed times and handle the Torah scroll and its gilded accessories with much respect. After a while she became bored. Her mother smiled blandly. Usually they came to the synagogue for a holiday or a bar mitzvah with its attendant interests and gossip. Now they were left with nothing but actual prayer.

We can go now, Hannah said.

Only if you want to, her mother replied, picking up her purse. It'll be Rosh Hashanah in a few months anyway, she added. She was descending the stairs back to Krystalgade and the other shops of the Latin Quarter even before the rabbi had returned the Torah to its place in the synagogue's ornate ark.

They stopped in a druggist's for her mother to buy an assortment of oddly-colored tinctures—migraine headaches were a regular feature of her life—and Hannah waited in the doorway, fingering through the small soaps and the bottles of smoked glass. She imagined a day of idle shopping ahead of them, or worse, an early return to their house and outright waiting for her father to return so they all might create the occasion of dinner. That was the extent of her next few hours, and she hated it. Until she remembered the address: Nørregarde. Of which Sofie had written.

In her letter Sofie described an ill-equipped group of young Jews, who met in a dingy apartment in this very neighborhood to debate Zionism. Sofie had attended only one or two meetings before her father made the arrangements that led them to Palestine. They will never get anywhere, Sofie wrote of these Zionists, since talk is the highest order of their existence. Still, it was just this lack of action that made Hannah think that, three years later, this same group might still exist at the address—somewhere here in the Latin Quarter—listed on the third page of Sofie's letter. And since she never felt further from Palestine than when she was in her well-tended house in Bellahøj, she thought she'd better look now, before she returned home.

As her mother emerged from the pharmacist's, Hannah roused herself to greet her and turned directly into the chest of a German soldier. She didn't so much bounce as skid off him, dropping squarely onto her tailbone and throwing her hands out to brace her fall. She felt the impact all the way to her teeth. She had landed on the rough stones of the street, a few feet from the sidewalk, and she felt the grittiness of tiny pebbles and other debris in her leg. The German wore a grey wool hat and a grey uniform unbuttoned at the throat and he was shorter than Hannah but as broad as two lesser men across the shoulders. He lifted her off the ground with one firm hand, placing it just under her armpit and pulling straight up as if opening a window.

As he lifted her the two other Germans also placed their hands on her as if to guide her. The stocky German said something like *Apologies* but Hannah couldn't tell if he said it in Danish or if she just followed the intent of his voice. He took his hands back and used them to adjust his rifle to its normal carrying position, pulling the strap across his chest, and it looked like a womanly gesture for all his bulk, like rearranging a handbag or purse. When she had finally brushed herself off all three Germans in their grey uniforms pointed her to the sidewalk as if giving directions to someone who had wandered just a few blocks off course. She looked to her mother who had crossed to her but stopped a few feet away. The Germans continued to point helpfully and Hannah wanted to say to them, You are the strangers here. Not me. But instead she walked dutifully to the sidewalk and brushed her dress again with a lank hand while the three soldiers nodded and turned and walked in the general direction of the cafés and shops of Gammel Square, just a few blocks away.

I think I want to go home, her mother said. And tucked her package under her arm.

But Hannah did not go home. Instead she walked down Nørregarde, a block of worn-down buildings just off the Latin Quarter.

Leaving my parents in a public place, she thought, is becoming a habit of mine.

It was a long street near the university, but so far in architecture and bearing from those large halls that it could comprise another city entirely. The comforting cafés and bookshops had disappeared, replaced by anonymous housing and few pedestrians. As she walked she passed no one. She unpeeled her letter in the middle of the street and read the address that Sofie described: 32 Nørregarde. The flat to the left of the stairs. She looked at that second phrase and thought, What does that mean? 32 Nørregarde was a squat, hunched building, only two windows on its face and a small door in the lower right corner, like a troll's entranceway or the servants' door to a long-unused mansion. She pictured entering that door and being confronted with any number of flats to the left of the stairs. She recalled her foray into Christianshavn just a few days earlier, the streets there so busy and noisy, and how easily she had moved through them, anonymous in that crowd. She pressed her hip with her right hand; it recoiled with tenderness from her fall. It would hurt badly tomorrow, and she hated Sofie Østenmuller for bringing her this close to actual Zionism and abandoning her here on this street, dangled on a clause of vague directions.

This would not do. She walked to the building, stood in front of that strange doorway for an uncomfortable length of time, placing herself far enough away from it as to indicate no particular commitment, but tipping her ear toward that door to hear some clue, positive or negative, that she had found the right place. She heard nothing. Then she backed away, retracing in reverse her approach to the building until she found herself on the corner again. She looked at the street plate on the nearest building—Nørregarde—and compared it to her directions as if she might have misread the letter this entire time. Of course she had not. She didn't walk down the street again but stayed at the corner, peering in the window of what appeared to be a dissolute shoemaker's shop. She felt it made a poor disguise for being here, since she couldn't even convince herself of interest in the cut-out soles, knobby shoelaces, and worn worker's boots that tottered across the face of the window display.

She peered in at the shoes while she contemplated what to do next. As she did so a young man who looked to be in his early twenties came around the corner. He had a long face and black curly hair that was cut too tight to his head, since it unfortunately exaggerated the features of his nose and his eyes. He carried a small wrapped parcel from a bakery near the university; Hannah recognized it by its packaging. He looked at her—there was no one else on the street—and she turned to him so that he had no choice but to stop.

What she meant to say was, Is this Nørregarde? Or, Could you direct me to 32 Nørregarde, which I understand is close to our current location?

What she said was, Are you Jewish?

He looked at Hannah with what seemed a lifetime of distrust and fear, mixed with a dab of abject puzzlement about how a German agent had been poured into the body of a skinny Danish girl.

Because I am, she added. Jewish. And she waved the letter in front of her.

His name is Aaron Marcus, and he says he can take her to Palestine. Hannah doesn't believe him, exactly. She's sitting in an apartment so small that the sum total of all its furniture would not equal one room of her house in Bellahøj. Not three-quarters of a room. Do people live like this? she thinks. It was like someone's bare suggestion of an apartment, a drawing where no one has bothered to fill in the details. There's one window in the tunnel-like living room, and it's crusted shut despite the summer heat.

I should leave right now, Hannah thinks. But she's surrounded by four people and they're all looking at her so she nods and takes a sip of something out of the dingy cup they've provided her and returns the cup to her lap and nods again.

What is your affiliation? Aaron asks.

Jewish, she says.

Aaron and the others all laughed. Of course Jewish, Aaron says. We're all Jewish. We're not talking about that.

What, then?

He proceeded to sketch for her a world so carefully configured that it outdid all of her university classes in its complexity. Communists, Socialists, Zionists, Bundists. Within the Communists some were Trotskyites, others not. And within the Zionists, there was Jabotinsky and there was Gordon. It was important to know these things, Aaron said.

Hannah listened to this long explanation, which Aaron delivered with an unflinching earnestness. He was not particularly handsome and it seemed like it had been a long time since he had eaten well. Hannah glanced furtively at the other people in the room. Already her world was expanding; here were Copenhagen Jews she had never seen before. Along with Aaron there was a man named Laurits, as blond and tall as any Jew she had previously met. And another named Michael, brown-haired and plain, like so many of the men Hannah knew at the university. There was a woman with dark, petite features and deeply set eyes. She said her name was Anise, a name that seemed far too exotic and frothy for the serious woman to whom it belonged. She made Hannah nervous just by sitting there.

Hannah returned her attention to Aaron when she heard him say the word Palestine. He was talking about a man named Gordon, a Socialist and a Zionist who, Aaron said, had uncovered the path for Jews to follow and had died tragically and heroically in its pursuit. Aaron said that he had come to respect Gordon in all ways and wished above all else to work on this man's farm in Palestine, sweating all day for the redemption of the land and pausing only to sit in the shade and read his words and drink them in thirstily. He smiled when he said this last phrase and looked to his companions who returned him nothing but blank looks. Don't you see? he said to them. How I take the old Jewish words and make them new by connecting them to Gordon?

At this the dark-haired woman sat up. She was very beautiful and had small furrows leading to her mouth, which made Hannah wonder about her age. She could be twenty-five or forty. When she spoke, though, the woman's voice was so light and girlish that it surprised Hannah.

Aaron, she said. Enough. The girl has just met us. Do you want to scare her off?

This brought the other men to a new level of attention. Laurits, in particular, stared at the woman with all the force of his tall body, as if the most wondrous thing he could expect was for her to speak another sentence of such perfect length and eloquence. He was plainly in love with her. Hannah, too, wanted to express gratitude that the woman had taken an interest in her. But when she tried to smile at her the woman turned away on her chair, back to her previous posture of indifference.

Of course, Aaron said. I'm sorry. Here, have something to eat. He pushed two shabby cakes at Hannah. She took one onto her lap, and, not wanting to eat it, found herself petting it instead, as if someone had just handed her a small, darling mouse. She stopped abruptly when she noticed what she was doing.

Is there anything? Aaron said. Is there anything you want to know?

Hannah looked at him. The light in the apartment had begun to thin and she thought of her father and mother, now sitting down to an early meal and wondering where their daughter might have been carried off to. I want to know about Palestine, Hannah said.

Of course, Aaron said. He looked to the others. Of course, he said to them. He got up from his chair and scurried off to what only could be his bedroom. He came back carrying a sheaf of maps, as if he would explain to Hannah the exact location of Palestine and how it was not, actually, right next to Denmark.

No no, Hannah waved at him. She put her cake down on the table so she could emphasize her point with both hands. I know *where* it is. What I want to know is, how are we going to get there?

Aaron looked at the others, then back at Hannah. He put down his maps. Go to Palestine? he said. That's not so easy. There's a war, he added, as if that particular news had perhaps not reached her house yet.

You are planning to go to Palestine? Hannah added quickly. She felt a sour taste in her mouth. She couldn't imagine going home again if this possibility had deserted her. She pulled her letter out of her pocket, began to unfurl it. Finally she just pointed to it. Sofie said . . . , she began.

Aaron put his hands up to stop her. Does he think I'm some sort of German spy, Hannah wondered, sent to uncover his little cell of Zionists? She smiled at the thought that this band of dessert-eaters might consider themselves dangerous, like the resistance the Germans deplored in their radio broadcasts and newspaper editorials. Perhaps it would be the subject of a paper bombing later in the week.

I don't know how to tell you this, Hannah said. She sat forward in her chair, looked at each one of them. I want to go to Palestine. She looked at Aaron. I want to go there, she said again.

Fine, he said. That's fine. He told her to return in a week, when they all would be meeting again to discuss the situation. I will not say I am planning to go, he said. Perhaps we will only talk about the hypothetical possibility. At this he turned his palms up and looked around the room, as if for the benefit of his invisible German handlers. Then he smiled at Hannah, and she thought he just might believe her.

On the way home she passed a cat sitting in the open doorway of a hardware store. The cat was brown and heavy and blinked at Hannah from its mouse-catching domain. In Palestine you would be a Jewish cat, she said to the cat. The cat walked off, indifferent.

7

the limits of human knowledge

Carl sat on a wooden bench at the Gilleleje train station, waiting for the train from Copenhagen. Two German soldiers stood next to the ticket booth, smoking cigarettes. There was a stack of boxes and some luggage to be loaded onto the train and next to that three crates packed with ice and cod. After a few minutes one of the soldiers threw his cigarette on the wooden planking and crushed it out with his boot and then began to finger through the cargo, reading luggage tags and tapping the boxes with the back of his hand.

Carl walked to the ticket booth and for the third time in the last hour asked the ticket taker what time he expected the Copenhagen train.

It hasn't changed, the man said. He applied a wine-colored stamp to a batch of tickets, leaving a mark like a bruise on the back of each one. When he looked up Carl was still standing there. I'll tell you if it changes, the ticket man said.

Carl stood for a moment more and the ticket man glanced over Carl's right shoulder at the German soldier inspecting the cargo. They won't find any bombs that way, the ticket man said. They put them on the tracks, out in the countryside. No one knows a thing about it until it's too late. He picked up his stamp and blew a piece of dust from it.

Carl lowered himself gingerly toward a bench. It took him a long time. He thought of a bolt he had tried to tighten in the *Jette* last night. His wrench had snapped off the head of the bolt, leaving a shiny, exposed spot. That's just what my back feels like, he thought. He rubbed his vertebrae absentmindedly.

The resistance had wrecked three cargo trains in the last week, two in Jutland, one right here in Sjælland, each carrying materials—grain, sugar, beer—destined for Germany. The noise from the explosions had shaken nearby farmhouses and dazed and bloody crewmen wandered through the fields, calling anyone, anyone, for help.

Cargo trains and passenger trains traveled on the same tracks. Sometimes just minutes apart. That would be an easy mistake to make, Carl thought. He found himself looking down the tracks, trying to will Jette's train into view. He sat there waiting for a long time; finally, the train edged around the corner, noisy and bearing the smell of machine grease.

From the very moment Jette stepped off the train he handled it badly. He could count back years before he remembered a time when he had spent more than twelve hours without seeing her, and in their everyday life their conversations—they were never extensive, they had no need to be—only picked up threads that had begun a few hours before. He could not imagine beginning a conversation from a dead stop. When he saw her get off the train, carrying her small bag, everything he thought to ask—about Copenhagen, about her sister, about the apartment where she stayed in Christianshavn—seemed so loud in his head, as if he were shouting to her across a large room. He would not do it. Instead he just stood there. Finally Jette asked how his back felt and he said fine and that lie made it harder for both of them. By the time they began to walk up the hill to their house the uneasiness had codified itself and taken on strength and dimension. He found himself looking at her in a purely mechanical way. He thought maybe she had colored her hair. Or perhaps the scarf around her neck was new. Either topic seemed immeasurably beyond him.

He had stewed some string beans and stewed some cabbage to accompany it and when they got to the house they sat at the pine table and ate that meager meal. He thought maybe Jette would cook something to add to it but she did not. Their table had nicks and grooves and Carl worked them with his finger. Then he speared a string bean and brought it to his mouth.

As they prepared to get into bed Carl took off all his clothes, pulling off first his socks and then taking down his trousers and underwear in one jerky motion. He wanted his wife, could not bring himself to disguise it. Jette was in bed and he rolled up next to her, hard already. She waited for a moment and then she turned onto her back and hiked her nightgown up in one stingy motion. He climbed on top of her, working his way right into it. Her skin was rougher than he remembered and now he was sure that she had done something with her hair because he could smell it, sickly sweet like one of the more common flowers, but he couldn't figure out which one. He strained harder and his back began to hurt. He thought maybe she liked it. She pushed her hips and her crotch against him, and he came quickly.

He woke from the cold in the middle of the night, still naked, shriveled. He opened their pine chest and took out two winter blankets made of thick wool. They were rough to the touch and pilled in his hands. Jette was asleep and just her head peeked out from the covers. He spread out the two wool blankets and put them over first his side and then hers until she looked very small under all of it, just a raised lump in their bed. Then he climbed back in, avoiding the damp spots on the sheets, and fell asleep.

Carl woke up thinking about money, how little of it they had. It was Sunday morning. He had dreamt that he was fighting with another man for control of a milk bottle, and when he woke it came to him that in his nighttime spasms he had grabbed first his pillow and then his wife's arm. When he let go he saw four red marks corresponding to the thickness of his fingers. She got up and, glancing only briefly at her arm, began dressing for church.

The itinerant pastor, hearing coughs and shuffles and the shifting of at least one handbag, quickly discarded his planned reading from Ecclesiastes on the limits of human knowledge and moved instead to the scene of Jesus at the sea. How Jesus called the fishermen into service. He moved simply and directly through the most familiar tropes, following the stolid path he learned in seminary from a succession of earnest, balding Lutherans, taking care to add some salient facts about the fish named after St. Peter, still caught to this day in that famous Sea of Galilee and enjoyed for its flaky, mild flesh.

He saw the eyes of a few of his congregants narrow with interest at these remarks, and, encouraged, the pastor offered some suppositions about the Sea of Galilee itself, its violin-like shape, its depth and temperature, leading them ever so carefully—slowly, now, they are not friendly to metaphors—toward their own water, the Oresund, which they could all hear through the church walls, splashing against the rocky beach, and, from there, to a vision of themselves as the very fishermen of Scripture, casting their nets into a cold sea and asking how they too might best serve the Lutheran Church.

It was his first incursion into a theme he planned to pursue over the coming weeks. He had gotten the idea while sitting in his lover's kitchen in Hornbæk, Gretta on her knees, uncurling his belt from its buckle, while he smiled stupidly at a photograph of her dead husband. There were pictures of the husband on every wall and table, including the one right there in the middle of the kitchen. Whenever the pastor looked at that photograph, a sepia portrait of a man in a borrowed suit, he felt as if he had caught the husband in the act of suppressing some very bad gas.

A strike! he had thought, as Gretta worked first the top button of his pants, then the next. She had very small fingers.

He would organize a strike among the Gilleleje fisherman. A small step, but if it caught on in the other towns, could hinder the flow of fish to German households. It was a good idea. No, an excellent one. The pastor had been looking for a way to distinguish himself in the eyes of the Church, which had grown noticeably colder in its support of the status quo and more forward in advocating for small acts of sabotage. If not a strike, then some kind of action. He would have to start now, warm the fishermen up to it. He looked with appreciation at the top of Gretta's head, down by his waist. He was ambitious, yes, and eager to make an impression on a population other than just rural widows. He pictured himself promoted to a pulpit in a large city—Arhus perhaps—then, on to Copenhagen. He could see Gretta's hair thinning along the ridge of her scalp, a pale furrow parting blond, wiry stalks. He didn't care. It just made her try harder to please him.

The pastor drew his sermon to a close and bore directly into a series of hymns, which the fishermen and their wives could carry with minimal effort. He stood at the front of the church, looked at the congregation from behind the small lectern afforded to the clergy, and picked out the men who were respected and thus crucial to his plan: Martin Borch from among the older men, Poul Andersen from the younger crowd. Carl Jensen was a possibility, though the pastor was wary of the man. He only indulged the walk up to the Viking graveyard out of affinity for Jette, who was a devoted and attentive member of the Lutheran Church. Besides, she was quite a delicious woman, despite the fact that she was fifteen years older than himself. And the pastor had long since reconciled himself to his attraction to older women.

But Carl knows, looking out into the Sound from the Viking graveyard, having left church at the end of the pastor's sermon, that the Sea of Galilee is not this sea, that it is fed not by the comforting baptismal waters of the Jordan but by some crackling ice sheet far to the north, and that no one—not even the Son of God—could walk on this particular water without drowning.

What point the pastor was to trying to make in his sermon, Carl doesn't know. He doesn't trust the man; he trusts fewer and fewer people these days. He watches Jette unwrap their sandwich from the greasy paper. Yesterday when she had gotten off the train from Copenhagen he knew her sister had renewed the offer to move down to Copenhagen—Really, Jette, what do the two of you have left up there but a beat-up boat and bad weather?—and that he would confront this in his wife's beautiful face all week.

But for now Carl stands in the Viking graveyard, accepts his bread and cheese sandwich from Jette, bends with difficulty to pick an aggressive weed from the stone that marks the fourth gravesite. He's waiting for the itinerant pastor to come up there so that they can have their short, polite conversation but it is the anniversary of Gustav Jensen's wife's death and so Carl expects that Jensen will keep the pastor down at the church a while longer. He had waited this way for the pastor before this one—a plump, wheezy Christian, his face red from the walk up the hill, a man with a taste for Jeremiah and heavily salted fish, who never failed to apologize to Jette for the heavy panting he attributed to the difficulty of climbing the hill—Carl had waited for him too. The wind shifts and Jette's skirt flutters against her legs and the sea smells fight with the manure and straw of town and Carl—thinking now of the First War when he was a young man and Jette a young woman and how they had waited, then, for the war to overtake them but it had never come, unlike now, when the war arrived almost before they knew it was happening, arching suddenly into fact like all the things in their lives—Carl misses, suddenly, the old pastor with his fishy breath and red face and easy humor about God, unlike the young itinerant pastor who walks up this hill and chats with Carl but always seemed to bring with him some subtle challenge to Carl's faith. Carl has outlasted all the pastors before this one, demanding that they walk up here for his audience, and he would outlast this one, too.

Jette smoothes her skirt with her hands. The days without her have been aching and lonely for him, especially the last, when he had come into town to wait for her train. He had sat on that wooden bench near the train station and watched the German soldiers—there seemed to be more of them, recently—on their commandeered bicycles and in their pressed uniforms, fitting so awkwardly into the local stores and at the café tables. Looking at a pair of young blond soldiers—boys, really—standing in front of the train clerk's window, Carl had the feeling, the first time this feeling had ever arrived to him, that he was seeing one of Jette's sons. The sons that had escaped Carl and Jette. He looked more closely at one of the soldiers, a corporal. The German boy had fine features, delicate like Jette's, set against the rough grey of his uniform, and gentle hands, even as he played the bolt on his rifle. Carl sat on the wooden bench, his hands trembling, and wondered why God—who had found no cause to provide Carl with a son, only a daughter born red and early and unbreathing and dead—had now sent his wife's unborn children to him in the form of an alien and invading army?

Carl thinks of this again as he bends to pick another weed from one of the Viking gravestones. Looking down the hill toward the Sound he thinks he sees the part-time pastor walking on to the dock where the fishing boats lay tied. But no, it's not him—though this man is young and thin like the pastor—and it is certainly no fisherman, either, because Carl watches the young man approach the wooden planking with cautious steps, as if he expects the dock to shift under his feet. Carl thinks that he should walk down there and investigate, despite the ache it would cause his back, but then Jette stands and takes his hand and leads him toward the path home. On the way up the hill to their house she tells him she is going back to Copenhagen.

8

1940

HER MOTHER AND FATHER AT breakfast at the weekend house. Hannah at sixteen. Pleasant, greasy smells of fried eggs carry through the house. Hannah can tell before she even arrives at the table that her father is the one who has cooked the eggs and that he has used thick pats of butter to do it. It's April, 1940, and Denmark has declared itself neutral in a war that has spiked business throughout the country. Bergstrom has been making vast quantities of paper and selling it all.

Her father decided at the last moment that Hannah would not go to school that week; he would not go to work. Instead they would go to their house in the countryside. The sudden decision, the quick packing—they give the sense that all this is stolen, and it feels so much sweeter for that. There's a famous castle not too far away, a sprawling fortress and estate built in 1629, and they may decide to visit it.

Hannah finishes most of her eggs, leaving just milky crescents on the plate. She brings it to the sink and peeks in on her parents in the living room of the house. The room has wide windows painted with a blue trim and offers a view into the neighbor's garden. Her father has found a radio and is trying to summon a football game. It's too early, though, so he clips it off and then forgets about it for the rest of the day.

Hannah has had a growth spurt. She's tall now, taller than her mother and nearly eye level with her father. It's good, she thinks, heading in the right direction, anyway, though her breasts have yet to catch up. She goes outside. She takes off her sweater, unclasps the top button of her shirt, bares her arms to the sun. It's new, this body of hers, and she's decided to see what it can do.

She takes a walk on the road leading away from town. The road signs point to fishing towns up the coast, Hellebæk, Hornbæk, Gilleleje. She's less than two hours from Copenhagen but from here the city seems like something made up, a story to frighten children. She lets her hand pass over the tall grass at the side of the road, then brings it down over the tops of the stalks until they tickle her palm.

She meets two boys on the path. They say they are seventeen, but they don't look that old. Their faces are angular and handsome. She can feel them admiring her. Their eyes float over her chest and down her waist and legs. One of them has a dog. He implores it to do tricks for her. The dog refuses. The owner grabs the dog by the muzzle, shakes it. The dog responds with a nip at his hand. Hannah laughs.

She decides that the flirtatious thing to do is to walk away, so she turns and lets them watch her as she goes.

Later that day Hannah and her parents are driving down that same road, heading back to Copenhagen. I forgot some papers at the office, was all her father had said, though Hannah suspects he has simply grown impatient with leisure. The castle would have to wait. It's already the afternoon and Bergstrom has planned to make it home by dinner, but they got a late start and her mother is put off. She feels rushed now, and she'll let Hannah's father know it the whole way back.

I'll have to call the maid back in, she says. I told her she could have the week.

So call her back in.

Hannah is in the back seat, head resting against the window. You don't like the country anyway, she offers, but her mother doesn't respond. The ride passes with little conversation, only mute landscapes moving by in the vernacular of house, barn, and field.

Suddenly her mother arches forward. Do you see something up ahead? she says. She leans closer to the windshield.

What is it?

There's a car pulled off the road.

There's dust churned up in front of them now and it's hard to see. Bergstrom slides the car carefully off the road. The right front tire crunches mustard-colored grass.

We'd better wait a minute, he says. He cranks down his window to see but there's dust everywhere and her mother complains that it's getting in the car. He rolls the window up, cups his hands over his eyes to see better.

There's more than one off the side, he says. Hannah can hear the growl of large engines and it doesn't seem to match the sound of their car or the two on the road ahead.

Bergstrom rolls down the window again and waves his hand to clear the dust. When he does they see a truck bear down the road and pass them, then another. The trucks are painted military grey and each has a black ornamental cross on the driver's door. The back of each truck carries German soldiers pressed shoulder to shoulder and the soldiers sway and bump each other as the trucks barrel up the road. There are many trucks and Hannah and her parents sit watching them until Bergstrom thinks to roll up the window, cutting away the dust and some of the noise, and then they sit and watch as still more trucks file up the road. When they've finally all passed Bergstrom cranks the key and they drive down the road, staring through the windows, past several more fields recently planted with wheat and then finally over the bridge into a city under occupation.

9

pauses among the bread and cheese

Bergstrom the papermaker sat in his study in Bellahøj, carefully constructing first the official accounting books for Bergstrom Paper, then the second, true set of books that he kept hidden in his mahogany secretary. His library, a broad collection of *halacha* and *aggadah* from all the famous sources, plus some more obscure ones, filled the entire left wall of the study. Though he rarely had time to read them anymore, he still, every few weeks, traveled across the canal to Christianshavn and deeper still, into the voluntary ghetto to buy the rare volumes that his contacts procured for him. They had become distinctly more available once the war began and more available still since the occupation. It was the first way the war had proven a bounty for him.

He envied the straight, green lines and the yellow columns of the ledger books, so clean and grid-like. The books received the numbers, simply accepted them. The books didn't wonder where the numbers came from. If he had possessed a more romantic temperament, he might've thought of the accounting books as lovers, the first as his wife, the second as his mistress, each waiting for the offerings that he brought them in terms of ever increasing sums and profits. But he did not think of them that way. He was faithful to his wife and faithful to his family. He wanted simply to fill these ledger books to the best of his ability.

What had begun years ago as a modest business creating quality letter paper, envelopes, and note cards for the upper class had, since 1940, become something else entirely. The Germans needed paper, vast quantities of it. In some ways, Bergstrom thought, the need to keep the German in paper seemed to rival his need for food, manpower, hard metals. They were obsessed with paper and the need to document every detail of their activities. Thus Bergstrom. He didn't ask where the pulp came from. He didn't ask where the paper went. He knew, and he didn't know. He didn't want to know. He took care not to look too closely. When the propaganda pamphlets dropped from the sky he avoided touching them, since he knew so well his own paper, its texture, its smell.

He knew his daughter was staying out late, wandering Copenhagen, declining to attend her classes at the university. Of course someone had called him. Hadn't he gotten her admitted? He would have to investigate that. He was convinced he had seen her wandering down the streets of Christianshavn, that low-rent district on the far side of the city. He would have to talk to her about that, at some point. But now he was busy. He was invaluable. He loved his family and wanted to keep them safe. If his wife and his daughter suffered from inattention in the meantime, he could live with that. The war would be over eventually. He would have time then to attend to all of the matters within his house. For now, the world was becoming larger all the time, and it needed him.

✢ ✢ ✢

When she brings out the food they sit, each regarding the other with curiosity. Occasionally she pauses among the bread and cheese and wrapped sandwiches to speak, pointing at the food as she does, as if naming things, as if she is just giving these items names. Her movements are careful and her face is soft, agreeable, the kind only a very young girl from his North Sea home would possess.

That morning a group of uniformed soldiers had entered the ghetto, fast on the heels of another load of paper from the sky. Like her they had pointed and named things, one among them marking down what his superiors had said. Watching them unseen from his alleyway he had thought once again of his brothers drowned, the smashed decanter, the whale oil dripping to the wooden floor, his mother's bleeding hand. After a while an old woman from the window above him emptied her garbage onto the soldiers below and they retreated, shouting, still marking. On the way out they shoved first an old man then a diseased beggar and overturned a clothes peddler's cart, which the clothes peddler gathered up again and righted dispassionately as if a brisk wind had simply come to vex him.

The Faeroe Islander looks at the girl before him, her face young, curious, so different from the women he knew in the Faeroes. He extends his hand to touch her and her skin is soft and smooth as the whale oil on its journey to the floor. They are standing now. She leans back, smiling, against the alley wall that he has insulated with paper. There is no hurry. He traces over her shoulder the swastika on one of the pamphlets then his hand wanders and he begins instead to trace her body. He feels in the walls the fire of 1794 and the fire of 1884, each of which ravaged Copenhagen to the edge of this building and retreated, the potential of which remains in these walls, hot, smoldering.

Why does he need—need!—to come here, he asks himself. To Nyhaven. The walk is far and each time he suffers a paper rainstorm. It's all his father's fault, he thinks. They almost left Denmark after all, back in the early twenties, when his mother still lived and his father traveled over the ocean, to America, one of a faceless Scandinavian wave fleeing the poor economy, the class ceiling, the oppressive sea. Thousands had stayed, but his father returned. I cannot abide America, he said. They have no public spaces. They do not want to see each other. They build their towns for speed. Everyone moves quickly, finishes his business, leaves. Or gets drunk. It's a stupid country, he said, dismissing an entire continent with a flick of his hand.

His father continued: Here, you take time. You sit. Anyone can sit. They talk about how democratic they are in

America, but here anyone can sit in Kongens Nytorv next to anyone else. Outside. How it's supposed to be.

To Bakman, remembering it now, this rant only confirmed his father's ridiculous view of history. For had not Europe, despite its celebrated public spaces where everyone sees each other, just emerged from one brutal, nasty war which involved a great deal of seeing each other for the purpose of murdering each other? And what now, except more of the same, with all the same basic players, one or two minor actors replaced, director fired, same stage, same theater, same war?

Still, like a vengeful spirit, his father's voice follows him, driving him out of his apartment and into the open, to Nyhaven, where he can see the boats and the canal, and the people and even the helmeted soldiers. It had reached the point where if he didn't see a soldier he felt uneasy, like a common still life in which the pitcher or bowl has been painted away. Now that was frightening.

✣ ✣ ✣

Hannah walked down the street to her friend Mari Bothke. A group of boys played soccer on a narrow street. The street was quiet and leafy and you would not know there was a war. Mrs. Bothke opened the door with a look of wonderment. Hannah, she said. Nice to see you. How are your parents?

Hannah said they were fine and entered the house. Its smells felt as familiar as her own bedroom: Mrs. Bothke's sweet perfume, the scent of baking, Mr. Bothke's pipe.

Mr. Bothke was a low-level civil servant in his everyday life, a Danish Nazi at home. He flitted from room to room like some brown-shirted ghost.

Mrs. Bothke shuffled to the kitchen to arrange a plate of treats. Hannah sat herself in the parlor, at the far end of which Mr. Bothke sat drinking a Carlsberg and examining the newspaper. If not for the uniform, he could be her father. He had never been friendly to Hannah and she took no particular offense when he ignored her.

Mari ran down the stairs and hugged Hannah before she even had a chance to get up from her chair. They hadn't seen each other for more than a year. If Hannah expected Mari to resent her for the absence, she was wrong. I'm sorry, Hannah began to say, but Mari shushed her and hugged her again.

They had been neighbors and friends since they were little children, sharing teachers and homework and eventually school-girl crushes. As a young girl Hannah could remember lying on the floor of that same parlor next to Mari, drawing elegant dragons and horses while Mari colored them in with her stubby fingers.

Since Hannah had started at the university, though, they had spent much less time together. Mari had been denied entrance to the university and had taken a job selling flowers at a kiosk at Radhudspladsen, in front of Copenhagen's famous city hall. During her first semester Hannah would walk down to Radhudspladsen and the two of them would stand in the shadow of the great building and eat their lunches, Mari having to put down her cheese and bread periodically to bundle a group of posies for a customer. After a while, though, Hannah fell out of the habit. The walk was long and she had to pass by so many soldiers to get there. When she did go, she was reluctant to talk to Mari about her classes—it seemed so rude, considering Mari's own status—and then, when Hannah stopped attending, what would she say? That she had discarded her place—the place that Mari had wished for—to spend time in a dank apartment plotting with other Jews?

Mrs. Bothke came back bearing coffee and a small assortment of cookies. I'm sorry to tell you, Hannah, we used our sugar rations up already this week, she said, as she poured the weak coffee into Hannah's cup.

That's okay, Hannah said, I think I'm starting to like it this way, and they all laughed. When Mrs. Bothke sat down, Hannah felt the need to be polite. How's Anders? she asked.

Mrs. Bothke reached to the table for a pile of letters. Shortly after the German occupation began, Anders went down to the German headquarters to volunteer for the Waffen S.S., his father standing behind him bearing a wide smile. He was not the only boy to do so. He's fighting the Communists, Mrs. Bothke said. Those squalid Russians, Mr. Bothke added from across the room, they'll kill every one of their own just to make sure our sons don't come home. Mr. Bothke took a drink from his beer and put it down.

Mrs. Bothke spread the letters from her son on the table in front of Hannah. She was a sweet woman with a splotchy face and she placed the letters with the care of someone arranging china for a dinner party, as Mari looked on. Hannah remembered Anders, could picture him well.

She had seen him swimming once, a thick-muscled boy with long legs. She had been thirteen then, splashing around with her schoolmates, and when he dove into the pool to join them she found herself wishing he would brush against her. Hannah looked at the letters, observed that the more recent ones had turned spare, the handwriting more elliptical. The last one was dated November, before the winter, nearly eight months earlier. We don't know where he is just this moment, Mrs. Bothke said. Somewhere in Russia. Mr. Bothke goes by 14 Læderstrade each day, but they can't tell him anything. 14 Læderstrade was the German headquarters. Mrs. Bothke added that they had given money to a clerk at 14 Læderstrade in the hopes that the man would make a special effort for them, but the man had been transferred away and they had heard nothing.

Hannah looked at Mari. I'm sure he'll be back soon, she said. Mrs. Bothke smiled, took a picture of him from her apron. He's a handsome boy, isn't he? Mrs. Bothke said.

All the girls liked him, Hannah said.

Mrs. Bothke gathered her letters and returned to the kitchen. Hannah pulled Mari close. I met somebody, she whispered. Mari looked at her expectantly. She was sweet, like her mother, and also splotchy. Hannah could see why people wanted to buy flowers from her.

Who? Mari said, A university boy?

A university boy had always seemed the definition of grandeur to Mari, something to admire like a museum painting. She couldn't imagine touching one. Hannah hadn't bothered to tell her about her actual encounters with men from the university; it seemed too painful and depressing.

He's not from the university. He's . . . But she couldn't decide how to finish the sentence. She wasn't even sure whom she had come here to tell Mari about. Aaron Marcus? The man in the fishing sweater, deep in his alley? What could she explain about that man? Understanding him seemed the least relevant fact of their relationship. She couldn't bring Mari to meet either of them, that was certain.

Yes, I met him at the university, Hannah said finally, and Mari clapped in response.

10

a wonder

Aaron and the others sat in the small living room, discussing politics. Aaron named a series of Danish governmental figures, all corrupt and complicit, he declared, in the current state of affairs. He had particular disdain for a minister who was a Jew. In Palestine, he said, such a man would not be tolerated.

Hannah, for her part, tried to imagine what events could prompt her to live in an apartment like this. A poor choice in marriage? An accident to her parents? She had a quick vision of her mother and father being run down by a truck in the street. The thought came to her easily—then it was gone. She looked around at the others, who had stopped talking and now looked back at her as if they could see what she had been thinking. She retreated to the kitchen and began washing dishes.

The light outside gradually disappeared from the kitchen and Hannah didn't bother to trip the light switch, so that after a short time she was rinsing dishes in the dark. Nonetheless she wiped down the sink and cabinets, going over them with the grey washcloth. Here's something I wouldn't do at home, she thought. She tried to clean with the ruthless efficiency employed by her family's various housecleaners over the years, but she couldn't replicate their strokes and instead let the rag drift about countertop. She turned to find Aaron standing in the kitchen, watching her. Again she felt embarrassed, as if she had been caught doing something illicit.

The others have gone, he said. Didn't you hear?

I was thinking, she said. I'll go now.

No, he hurried to say.

Aaron told her how much he respected her ideas on the Jewish National Home, its eventual form and culture. That he, like her, envisioned a society in which all workers, irrespective of their labor, turned over their income to a central committee. This last statement she recognized as directly quoted from a pamphlet he had read aloud at a Zionist meeting two weeks earlier. He told her how he had volunteered for six brutal months of farm training in Jutland, before the war, so that he might contribute to building of the Land. It gave him a new appreciation for the plight of the worker, he claimed. Still, he looked as if he had rarely seen the sun.

If nothing else, Hannah thought, he has an opinion on what it means to be Jewish. Its burdens and implications. It was a subject she had never held an opinion about before meeting him.

Aaron rushed through his sentences and stared at some vague point on her body. She imagined him practicing the whole speech in front of a mirror, perhaps aloud. Also, he added, pausing to pick an invisible thread from his trousers, he found her beautiful. She knew this to be not quite true, though she thought she compared favorably to most of the women he encountered.

Would you . . . ? he began. Then he kissed her, his hand reaching for her right breast.

I guess it's about time, was all she thought.

He hurried her out of her clothes and she found herself feeling cold, much colder than she would have expected. She wished for a blanket. Not out of shyness, but because she felt sure the skin on her thighs and arms had raised up from the chill. Couldn't he feel it? She felt like a plucked chicken.

They moved from the kitchen doorway to the couch where the others had so recently been sitting. She tried to focus on Aaron but her own body kept getting in the way. It was so long and difficult to manage. When Aaron moved on top her leg jerked up. She was sure she had kneed him hard in the ribs, or the stomach. Then she tried to just lie flat but they bumped bone on bone like plates clattering against each other. She mumbled an apology but he seemed not to hear, since he had busied himself with some part of her chest.

This body—the same one which Aaron was pursuing so fervently—had arrived to her nearly seven years before, but she still didn't know it nearly as well as one might hope. It had started to change in earnest at age thirteen, during a period in which she attended several bar mitzvah ceremonies in successive weeks at the Copenhagen synagogue. I think we're going to need to have some new dresses made for you, her mother said, as Hannah stood in her underwear in her bedroom early one Shabbat morning. Her mother held up one dress with a prim, off-white silhouette. Hannah had worn it just once, a month earlier. This one might not even reach your knees anymore, her mother said, laughing. It did, in fact, fall to mid-calf, but the implication was clear.

This was on a November morning and the light in her bedroom was still dim with the onset of the day. Hannah could barely see as far as her own dresser. On her nightstand she kept a collection of miniature glassware bought at Tivoli. Circus clowns and such. In the filtered morning light they looked like ghosts.

At the bar mitzvah that day she watched the boy, Avram, dull and pink-faced, ascend to the reading of the Torah. His father draped him in a brilliant blue-and-white *tallis* ordered special from Germany. Avram's mother and grandmother beamed down at him from the women's section and looked around in expectation of congratulations.

Hannah felt a grinding envy each time she witnessed the *tallis* unfolded over another boy. What did she get? Certainly no ceremony—that was for boys only. All she received, quietly and relentlessly, was a tall, awkward body that towered over the boys her age. Some of them still hadn't caught up. You'll fill out, her mother told her, when she saw Hannah staring at her reflection in a dinner plate. She had, but indifferently. Instead, even now, when she looked at herself in her hand mirror, she saw a flat chest, small nipples. One time, glancing quickly, she thought for a moment that a naked boy had found his way into her room.

How had she been shaped before that? She couldn't quite remember. Her mother would sometimes joke with Hannah about the round belly she had as a baby—apparently she was a fat child. Or maybe it was just the spherical, air-displacing stomach that all small children had. Now she wanted it again. It seemed so easy to move through the world that way, using that round belly for ballast, like a wide-bottomed boat. She wanted that simple, pre-pubescent body back now, as she tried to arrange herself with Aaron. He smelled of print and paper, and it reminded her of her father.

✠ ✠ ✠

What's wrong with you? Henrik says. He and Bakman are sitting in the hospital cafeteria, drinking stale coffee and picking at the remnants of a pastry. They had just finished a game of chess; Henrik had mated Bakman with a queen-bishop combination of fewer than twelve moves.

Nothing's wrong, Bakman says. It's been a long shift.

You can't fool me, Henrik says. There's something wrong *in there.* He reaches over and taps Bakman on the temple. Colleagues, he says, spreading his arms, here we have the puzzling case of young Dr. Bakman. Two female doctors at the next table pause, forks by their mouths, to stare. This is Henrik's *We're on rounds* routine, and Bakman has never found it amusing.

Young Dr. Bakman, Henrik announces, is often distracted. Witness the pupils: grey, dilated. Witness the lack of sophisticated thought. Beaten by an obvious queen approach. Witness the lack of response *down there,* or so they've been saying at the nurses' station.

Cut it out, Bakman hisses.

Cut it out. Cut it out. Really, Bakman. I think you're suffering from a fatal ill humor. You should write yourself a prescription for some of the more potent pharmaceuticals.

I want to leave, Bakman says.

Leave the hospital?

Leave the country. Leave Denmark.

And go where? There's a war on, don't you know. It's quite everywhere now.

One of the doctors, a grey-haired cardiologist, passes by the table. He nods at Henrik, walks away without acknowledging Bakman. Bakman waits for him to go, then clutches Henrik by his lab jacket. Watch the sleeve, Henrik says, I just had this pressed.

What's going on here? Bakman says.

What are you talking about?

You know what I'm talking about. What's going on here? Why all the mysterious looks? Why all the sudden activity down at the morgue?

The only one here fascinated by the morgue is you, Henrik replies. And we haven't even talked about that particular curiosity.

There's something going on here, Bakman says. He still has his grip on Henrik's sleeve. There's some resistance crap going on, isn't there? Isn't there?

I thought the resistance didn't interest you.

There's something going on here. Something. And I'm the only one who doesn't know about it. I'm the only one. Everyone else is in on it, aren't they. He grabs Henrik by the lapel, pulls him close. Aren't they?

Henrik pauses, fixes Bakman with cobalt eyes. He smiles. Yes, he says.

In the gloomy light of the apartment Hannah told Aaron of the foreman's suicide. She began by biting into a cake Aaron had purchased on the Strand, but it betrayed its day-old status in all its dry and crumbling edges. It seemed in fact a cake aimed at creating the greatest dehydration possible in the mouth of one who would try to eat it, some last revenge on behalf of all cakes as it was swallowed. She put it down.

I don't know why I'm telling you this, she said. It happened nearly two years ago.

Peter Sørensen seemed, Hannah said, a resolutely ordinary man. He lived in a modest house north of Amalienborg. Not a fashionable part of town, but a useful one, rents manageable, a modest bicycle ride from her father's factory. Even when he made foreman he kept his family there, as if he merited no improvement in his standard of living despite his greater income. He had risen to foreman of the factory floor not through his brilliance or innovative qualities but by his steadiness. He's as regular as a clock, her father would say. Her father promoted him hoping that his inherent punctuality would somehow insinuate itself into the minor workings of each machine, the gears meeting each other at each precise moment, like Sørensen himself drinking his coffee or Sørensen himself putting on his coat and departing the exact minute he completed his day's work. For the most part it worked, and Bergstrom said on more than one occasion that paper flowed from his factory like water since Sørensen's promotion.

He had seemed, Hannah said to Aaron, to have reached all that to which he aspired. His wife had efficiently born three children, all boys, at precise intervals of two years separate. Two blond, one brown, Hannah added. Then the occupation. Something about it drove him to gloom. He kept his hours, but with less than his usual concentration. Her father even had call to chastise him once, in the big office overlooking the factory floor. That had never occurred previous in all their years of association.

This is the puzzling thing, Hannah said. He hardly had cause to even see a German soldier. If he had closed his eyes the whole occupation at that time might have seemed a dream, a faint memory shrugged away by morning coffee. In retrospect, she said, he seemed most vexed by the idea of it. Not by its factual implications.

The event itself occurred one evening after he had put the three boys to bed. It seemed so in character, Hannah said. Putting in a whole day's work. Other people would commit suicide in the morning and save themselves the labor of the day. The boys slept in two beds in a single room, the two younger ones bunked together and the third just a body width separate. He went downstairs and paused at the kitchen, where his wife washed the dinner dishes. She's a pretty thing, Hannah said. Not that that explains anything. He said to her, Do you smell something? and pinched up his nose twice as if testing the air. No, she said. I do, he answered, and descended to the basement.

She heard him banging around down there. Called down, You all right? He called back, Yes. Everything's fine. She heard more banging, tapping, a clang. She called again and again he responded. She washed each dish in their cramped sink and then dried it each in turn while the next one soaked. That was her way about it. When she finished she hadn't heard him tapping around down there for some time and neither had he come back up the stairs. She decided to test the situation for herself. When she cracked open the basement door a rush of gas came so pungent and metallic that she nearly passed out right there on the top step. She backed out shaking and rang for the police.

When the police arrived and investigated the basement they discovered next to the foreman's body a strange arrangement of gas pipes and rag tie-offs, a maze of intricacy and sophistication for the specific duty of delivering enough gas to choke off a person's breathing. He seemed to have in mind an automatic device for suicide, based on some early industrial vision, that would shut itself off after his death. The still rank odor of heating gas which hung about, even with every available window cracked open, threw a shadow on his abilities. Also one could see in the piping false starts and dead ends. It took him some time to get it right. Clumsy, you see, in the ways of suicide. And he pursued his task with using a mass of wrenches and pliers such that it made the policeman sorely amazed that no accidental strike or flinting sent the whole family to an explosive death. It's a wonder, he said.

11

farmhouses and sectioned fields

One week after confronting Henrik at Bispebjerg Hospital Bakman found himself on a train to North Sjælland, into the countryside above Copenhagen. It was his first errand for the resistance. I need you to go on a trip, Henrik had said to Bakman down in the morgue, where Bakman had been performing the twice-weekly duty of cataloguing the derelict and unclaimed of Copenhagen.

There's a fishing town in the north we want you to look at, Henrik had said. Basic matters: geography, general character of the place. Number of Germans. Bakman was to make copious observations but write down nothing.

For what?

Henrik wouldn't say.

Are you looking at all the fishing towns up there, or only Gilleleje?

Henrik wouldn't say.

Fine, Bakman had said. Fine. Come help me with this.

Together the two of them rolled an extremely heavy dead man onto his side, while Bakman checked for distinguishing marks on the man's back, buttocks, thighs. The man, though dead, kept wanting to flop back into a resting position. Bakman had to lean into the fleshy part of the man's backside to prop him up.

What would you say that is? A horse? Bakman pointed to a greenish shape on the man's lower back.

A parrot.

A parrot? Bakman poked at the mark with his finger, then grabbed a handful of the skin and stretched it out like taffy, trying to determine the tattoo's intent. I'll call it a bird, he said. They let go and the dead man fell to the gurney. He seemed to gasp.

Four hours later, when his shift was over, Bakman boarded a train from Copenhagen heading through the central town of Røskilde to Gilleleje on the North Sjælland coast. He understood that there would be no reimbursement for the train, the room in Gilleleje, or any miscellaneous expenses. Already the resistance was costing him money. The train passed like water through the membrane of Copenhagen, entering a repeating, numbing landscape of damp fields and humorless small towns.

A half-hour into the trip a white-haired couple entered Bakman's cabin. He searched the cabin from top to bottom to locate a polite way to keep them out but found none. The man settled himself in the cabin, explained to Bakman that he had worked thirty years for the city of Copenhagen, and proceeded to tell Bakman of every inequity visited upon him over those thirty years. Outside the sky was grey and it resolved every feature of the landscape into a general blur. Bakman had the brief pleasure of watching a cow take a long, soggy dump.

The man said his name was Gruenwald. His wife removed two canning jars from her bag, opened one of them. It smelled rancid. Gruenwald took one of the jars from his wife and held it in the air as if proposing a toast. Bakman, horrified, thought that the man was going to drink directly out of the jar. Instead he reached into the jar and pincered out a wiggling pickled vegetable. He ate it in two moist bites and wiped his hands on his trousers.

The man tipped the jar in Bakman's direction. No, thanks, Bakman said. I just ate, he added uselessly.

He found half a cigarette in the inside pocket of his pea coat and considered smoking it. More small talk. When the couple learned that Bakman was a doctor they told him a long, interminable story about their son, who had died fifteen years earlier from a rheumatic condition. Farmhouses and sectioned fields slid by the train window. Bakman agreed that it sounded like a tough case, that even with the progress in medicine it would have been difficult to avoid the worst.

Yes, the mother said. Nothing could be done. I knew it from the beginning. Nothing could have been done.

He was our only son, the man said.

They sat in silence for a time. Bakman smoked. When their stop came the man said to Bakman, This country will be looking up again soon. Just you wait. Denmark will rally, as if Denmark needed just a few healthy players to turn its season around. The woman insisted that Bakman keep their second jar. It was filled with a milky white substance surrounding grey squares and had all the features of herring, at last as far as Bakman was willing to investigate. He stashed it under the seat as soon as they left the cabin.

Bakman only had a few minutes to himself before two teenagers burst into the cabin and threw themselves against the seat in a tousle of legs and arms. They each had red, splotchy marks on their neck indicating some recent adolescent sexual activity. The boy's blazer bore the fanciful crest of Søro Academy, a place that figured large in his father's rantings against the clubby educational practices of Copenhagen's upper classes. The boy was fine-boned and handsome and the girl was fine-boned as well, dressed in a simple white blouse and a grey skirt that descended only as far as the tops of her knees. As soon as they sat down they began to grope each other, with Bakman as witness.

The Søro boy kissed the girl with such enthusiasm and penetration that Bakman thought he was trying to remove something from her throat, possibly with his tongue. Bakman strained desperately to suppress the need to cough. He could not. He felt it rise up in him until he barked something from halfway up his lungs. It came out as a puff of grey smoke and an odd smell.

The girl looked at Bakman and giggled, covering her mouth with her hand. The boy skewered Bakman with a look. Then he took his blazer and formed a little tent over himself and the girl, hiding the two of them from the waist up. Soon Bakman could hear the sounds of wet kissing, rapacious hands, more giggling.

Oh God, Bakman thought.

He put his head against the window and thought of ways to sabotage Henrik's medical career. He fell asleep. The train stopped abruptly and the young couple was gone and Bakman stumbled off, squinting at a white sign hanging from the side of the ticket booth. GILLELEJE. There was nothing else around, only a line of small buildings in the distance huddled together like sheep. He dragged his one piece of luggage down a dirt road toward the town. For all Bakman knew the trip itself could be a hoax, a diversion, a false trail. It wouldn't be past Henrik to send him on a fool's errand. He didn't even know what he was looking for.

The next morning Bakman stood on a narrow street in Gilleleje, wondering how to proceed. He had spent the night in a cramped room above what seemed to be the town's only pub. He had offered to share the room, to limit expenses, but the pub owner, a small man with a peppered beard, had waved at the empty hallway and replied, Do you see anyone else waiting for it?

He woke early. He ate a simple meal of bread and fish in the pub's empty room, the smell of beer emanating from the wooden tabletop. Then he wiped his glasses on his shirt and went out into the harsh morning light of the town.

He felt the heaviness of the salt air on his skin, a chemical process. The Fishermen's houses proceeded in a line down the street, each a different height and size, like poorly cut boards. Everything about Gilleleje was small. Even the houses stood close together, as if wishing to occupy as little of the world as possible. They were painted a variety of colors, dried peach, muddy red, aqua, but all had faded and cracked as if left too long in the sun. Each house had the year of its construction marked in cast iron numerals above the doorway in what struck Bakman as a desperate attempt to be taken seriously. They were old, he had to give them that.

Where to start? Just look around, Henrik had said. Lacking any particular method, Bakman found himself thinking of the town in terms of an autopsy. Cause of death? Currently unknown. However, asphyxiation is standard in cases like these.

He walked down a street of uneven stones, grass poking generously through the spaces, the houses all withered organs. The occasional bicycle lay propped against a wall.

At the corner of a street named Vestrogade he came upon what appeared to be a market or general store, actually a listing square of timber and brick with an old Tuborg poster as its sole decoration. On the poster, a plump, balding man in jacket and tails stood by the side of the road under a hot sun, wiping his forehead and dreaming of the restorative properties of beer. Bakman decided to enter.

He opened the door to find a grey-haired man behind the counter, staring reproachfully in Bakman's direction. Hello, Bakman said. The man nodded in return, employing a forehead so large Bakman immediately suspected some kind of hydrocephalic condition.

The store contained enough racks and shelves to suggest that it once contained a vast library of goods, but the war had reduced it to a sorry collection of items. Handwritten signs offered prices for nonexistent goods in kroner and Deutsche marks. The prices had been blotted out and rewritten a number of times to compensate for the rampant inflation and changing exchange rates. Dusty cans sat on shelves like survivors of a previous civilization. In one wooden box a group of misshapen zucchini kept company with two oozing tomatoes. There was only one customer other than Bakman, a blond woman. She was small and pretty. She placed a few goods—two onions, a can of sugar beets, a small wrap of lamb—in front of the grocery man and stood counting ration cards.

Bakman inspected the shelves with a conspicuous interest, picking up cans and rotating them in his hand, foraging through the vegetables. Then he turned to face the front of the store. I'm from Copenhagen, he said, to no one in particular.

The blond woman and the grocery man looked up from their counting. The grocery man pulled three strands of grey hair across his forehead, caravans crossing a wide and unforgiving desert. They then looked down again.

I hear there's some kind of old church here, Bakman said. He couldn't remember where he had heard that. The woman piled her purchases into a brown bag made of burlap or some other rough material. Is anybody there today? Bakman asked.

It's Monday, the grocery man said. He shook open a newspaper, made a show of reading it.

Bakman returned to his inspection of the store. At the front, in a glass case, the grocery man had put out an assortment of *smørrebrød*. Lacking the inclination to buy grocery paper, he had set the sandwiches on whatever kind of paper was available, newspapers, old book pages, propaganda pamphlets. Bakman selected one with three pink shrimp curled on a pale scrap of lettuce. The grocery man handed it over, pamphlet and all. Behind the counter there was a case of beer, the bottles label-less and dark. It was nine o'clock in the morning. Bakman bought one anyway.

He left the store, sandwich in one hand, beer in the other, to find the blond woman waiting for him on the street.

I'm Jette Jensen, she said.

His hands were full and, lacking any other way to be polite, offered his name.

The woman had blue eyes to accompany her blond hair, and networks of burst capillaries at her cheekbones that stood out against her pale skin. It was the only real element that suggested her age, but it did so efficiently. She could not be mistaken for less than forty. She had pinned her hair back in an entirely practical manner, and Bakman could see wisps of grey among her roots.

I can take you down to the docks, she said. Some people like to go down there when they visit, she added, though Bakman could not imagine who in the world that might be. He was struggling to finish his sandwich, since the lack of a free hand was making him feel terribly handicapped, even to manage this simple conversation. The church is on the way, she said.

Okay, he replied. If nothing else, he would now have something to report to Henrik. He finished the sandwich and followed it with a pull on the beer. It had the spicy flavor of some sort of home brew, heavy with malt. It either contained no alcohol or a great amount of it. He decided to drink the beer further to find out.

They began walking and she asked where he lived in Copenhagen. He told her Nørrebro, which she received with a blank look. My sister and brother-in-law live in Christianshavn, she said.

Ah, Bakman said. He didn't know anything about Christianshavn and didn't have anything to say about it. Then he remembered that his father's watch shop had been near that neighborhood, but he hadn't been in the area for many years and so he couldn't, he told Jette, attest to what it might be like.

It is my plan to go and live there, she said abruptly. They were walking toward the center of town and the houses had grown even more closely pressed together, though Bakman would not have thought such a thing possible. He took another drink of the beer. He was happy to have it.

My husband does not believe we can afford to live there, she said. Maybe he's right.

Bakman agreed that it was expensive in Copenhagen, even for himself, a doctor. Well, a medical student, he corrected.

You work in a hospital?

Yes, he said. He felt on surer ground now.

She sat with that for a few minutes as they walked. She pointed out the full, round body of the church, by far the largest building in town. Bakman said that it seemed quite nice. Beyond the church he could see first the beach and then the water, grey as mercury and sloshing against the shore.

Can a woman have a baby after a miscarriage? she asked.

Sure, Bakman said. I've seen it happen.

How about after three miscarriages?

Well, Bakman said. That's unlikely. It suggests some congenital abnormality of the uterus or, maybe, a circulatory problem. The woman would have to avoid all activity, and even then—

From the stricken look on the woman's face Bakman realized that she had been talking about herself. It's not recommended, he added.

Oh, she said. I see.

She reshuffled the contents of her grocery bag to make for easier carrying, and then smoothed back a few strands of long blond hair that had sprung loose from her pinnings. I thought the doctors in Copenhagen might be somewhat more capable than the ones found here, she said.

I imagine so, Bakman thought. He had nearly finished the beer and had found it hadn't at all produced the effect he had sought. He was painfully sober.

I do recall seeing some discussion of the subject in the medical journals, Bakman said. He couldn't remember the last time he had actually read a journal, but it seemed as reasonable a tack as any. He threw out the names of several drugs she would never remember. Then he found her looking at him with such riveted interest that he became afraid that she actually might. These are experimental treatments, he added.

She nodded at this as if experiment were the best one might hope for in the current world. We're almost at the docks, she said, and they began walking again. The air began to smell of fish. They passed low-slung storehouses with boxes piled beside them. At a small icehouse a group of mangy cats scratched at a board, eager at the prospect of the fish inside. As Bakman approached one cat turned and hissed at him with such feral aggression that he jumped back. The woman kept walking.

Here it is, she said.

A series of docks jutted out into the Sound. Small boats swayed in each available space like ornaments. That's my husband's boat, she said, pointing to one.

It was a small, blue-hulled boat with *Jette* written near the stern in bright paint. It was not much bigger than a man's bed. He goes out in that? Bakman declared.

The woman shrugged. That's Sweden, she said, pointing to something far on the horizon, across the water. All Bakman could make out was a brown shape, a rubbing at the bottom of the sky. Everything above it was blue and sharp and Bakman found it difficult to fix his eyes against that clarity of sky.

If my husband doesn't agree to move to Copenhagen I will go alone, the woman said. They were both looking at Sweden and Bakman thought she had mistaken it for Copenhagen. He didn't know what to say.

Thank you for the walk, was all he could come up with.

Thank you, she said. Then she turned and followed the path back up the street they had just come down together.

He waited there until she was long gone, reclaimed his bag from the pub and boarded the train to Copenhagen.

He viewed, in reverse order from when he came, the fields, farmhouses, groups of cows. When he reached under his seat to stash his coat he found the jar of herring still sitting there.

12

1915

When the circle of boys finally backed off the girl Carl found himself the closest to her. He was near enough to touch her. Most of the boys had moved to the barn's entrance and now stood together, drinking from an open flask. Carl bent toward the girl. He could hear windmill blades cranking around in pace with the wind. They turned unevenly and the noise grew louder and softer, a needle moving over a warped record. The girl huddled below him on a thin smattering of straw. Her skirt was bunched at her thighs and with one hand she struggled to free her *underlinnen* from its tangle at her ankles. Her thrashing had scattered the straw and so she sat mostly with bare skin against old cow-feed grains and cold dirt.

She was not by any standard a pretty young girl. In the flickering light of the barn's lamp she seemed well proportioned enough, until you saw her face. In the space between her nose and mouth she had a great harelip, a cleft like a knot in wood. It ran from her teeth to her nostrils and divided her face into two uneven halves, both ugly. Looking at the cleft, and the girl so worn and pathetic sitting on barn floor, Carl wished that when she was a young child someone had taken that slit between thumb and finger and pressed it together until her skin of itself had seen the wisdom of joining back together. Failing that, glue or some other substance, anything.

Of course this was why they had picked her. Her ugliness made her unused to flattery and when two boys came upon her on the road and invited her to a party in Mortensen's hay barn she giggled and agreed go with them.

It didn't happen right away. First she stood there, uncomfortable, alone amongst ten local boys. One of the boys made a half-hearted attempt to seduce her, reaching for her hand, but she pulled away from him. He moved toward her until she was cornered and pressed her to the ground and the others gathered to watch.

Carl had drunk enough homemade liquor to feel warm despite the chilly weather. He had laughed when the two boys brought the girl in, saying, Look who happened by on the road. Then he stepped outside to smoke a cigarette and when he came back in two circles had formed, one around the girl and the other with boys drinking and talking about agricultural matters and how hard their fathers worked them. Carl joined this second group. He too thought his father worked him too hard. By then the second circle had widened to join with the first and somebody tugged on Carl's sleeve and said, Your turn. When he did not move right away another boy stepped in front, a blond boy with awkward hands who worked on a nearby pig farm.

But Carl had watched them, her legs kicking against the dirt, someone's hand clamped over her mouth. He was still standing near her while the circle of boys took up residence in the corner of the barn. One held his hands to the lamp, rubbing his palms together and then placing them against the lamp glass and then rubbing them together again.

Help me stand up, the girl said. Help me stand up, she said again, loud enough for everyone to hear. With a rough jerk he pulled her to a standing position. He felt the awkward bulge in his pants and he looked to her for a sign that she had noticed it too but she gave him none. She ran out the door, one hand pressed over her skirt. As she left one of boys laughed but the others just stayed quiet. One troubled the dirt with his boot. They reminded Carl of the way football players stood together in the rain, saying nothing but clumped next to each other anyway, eyes fixed on the ground or on the next man's cleats.

All at once he felt the lateness of the hour, the chill, damp weather outside and the lonely dark way back to his house. There all would be asleep including his sister, who spent most evenings banging out scratchy tunes on a reclaimed piano and whose awful musicianship sent Carl to seek the company of others.

As Carl made to leave he realized that the group had struck upon a new topic of interest and enthusiasm and that the topic was himself.

You too good for her? one said to Carl.

They moved toward him, an Ishmaelite progression. They stood between Carl and the door, a line of young men irregular as a worn fence but with no obvious gap for escape. Through the open barn door Carl could see the woods casted by moonlight. He could see tree trunks, thick at their bases but gradually vanishing as they rose toward the dark so that the mind had to construct the continuation of branches, their shape and attitude. Every few moments a shadow obscured the entire scene of trees as the blades of the windmill turned over them. As they turned the blades creaked a mournful creaking and Carl thought once again of his sister's piano playing, this time with more affection.

Carl was big even at that age but there were many of them and most older than him. They gathered closer. One of them, Martin Lund, had married the week before. Carl thought Martin's young wife very pretty and he also knew that being pretty had little to do with anything related to this evening. One of the Mortensen boys to whom the barn belonged spoke. Yeah, he said. He's too good for her.

Fuck you, Carl said.

Then they were on him. It took a long time. When it was done blood dripped from Carl's nose and his right ear felt hot, burning. Carl felt it with his hand and found that it was not made of hot coals—as he would have expected—but cartilage and flesh, though so bubbled and swollen as to feel nearly unrecognizable as a part of himself. His ribs ached from where they had kicked him. His tongue seemed to take up a larger place than usual in his mouth and was surrounded by strange, metallic tastes. His body felt altogether a dumb weight. The first time he tried to stand his knees buckled and something went wrong in his back and he stayed awhile on his hands and knees like a supplicant. The second time he tried to stand he was more successful. He prepared himself for them to come at him again but they did not. He stumbled out into the dark.

When he finally arrived home he did not try to climb the stairs but instead sat down at the kitchen table, a sitting position giving the least offense to his ribs and back. He slumped a bit. Sometime in the night his mother came down to load the woodstove. She wore a flannel nightdress that covered her down to her ankles and she looked thin and delicate. When she noticed Carl at the table she just continued about her brief business. If she noted his condition she gave him no sign, fights being a common way for boys to measure each other and respected for their educational value.

This was in late fall. Soon the weather turned and they packed in to their houses to last out the winter and so all the barn company had little opportunity to encounter one another. In the spring the cold broke and Carl accompanied his father to town to pick up supplies. He was standing outside a store when the harelip girl came around the corner of the building so fast she almost bumped into him. She looked at him and then continued on her way without saying a word. As she walked away Carl's father came out of the grocery carrying dried provisions and a small box of German chocolates. He had opened the box and his chin betrayed a smear of caramel. When he caught a glimpse of the girl walking down the street he said to Carl, I hear she likes the boys. Often it's your less attractive ones. And he grinned.

Carl left a week later. He carried all his belongings in a satchel and had stolen his father's pocketknife. It bulged in his pocket like an erection.

13

clowns in half-masque

Hannah walked to the factory gate, taking care to step over and around the pamphlets that littered the ground like a wintry slush. They had been falling all during the walk from her house in Bellahøj—it was a long walk—and had stopped just as she got near the factory. As she approached she saw four of her fellow Zionists loitering at the big iron gate, shuffling in their coats like workers awaiting their shift. When Aaron Marcus saw her coming he turned and shook the gate.

When she got closer she could see that there were in fact only three Zionists she recognized along with one woman she had never seen before. Michael Oppenhejm, the plain, brown-haired young man, stood next to Aaron. He had shaved just that evening and his face was smooth and pink. It looked as soft as her mother's best sheets and though she had never been attracted to Michael, Hannah found herself wanting to reach out and touch his cheek, to see if it was as pleasant as she imagined.

Anise stood with another woman just apart from Aaron and Michael. This woman had her head against Anise's chest and their arms were wrapped around each other. They could be sisters—they were both so pretty—but the friend had blond, nearly white hair in the way of Danes who were not in any way Jewish. They held each other in a way that gave Hannah pause.

They all five were standing in front of a factory in Christianshavn. Somewhere in the nearby streets lived the man with the fishing sweater but it was a very late and dangerous hour and Hannah didn't dare try to find him. Besides, she was busy with something else tonight. She was trying to find a way to Palestine.

They were next to the Copenhagen Naval Yard, a large complex of warehouses, dark now all the time, built along Copenhagen's main canal. It was directly across from here just a few months ago—just on the other side of the canal—that she had stood in Nyhaven, wishing she could walk across a bridge of water to Palestine. She now realizes that if such a bridge existed it would have carried her only directly to Christianshavn.

When the Germans came in April, 1940, this naval yard hosted much of the military fleet of Denmark. When news of the German invasion reached the naval yard the workers here immediately went about scuttling the ships, placing bombs in their holds like pockets of honey in a beehive. Hannah and her family had heard the explosions all the way up in Bellahøj. When she looked at the dark warehouses of the naval yard it was as if no ships had existed there now or in any previous time. Still, she knew their wreckage was there somewhere, underwater.

Aaron shook the gate again and in response a watchman came out from the inner yard of the factory. Despite the August heat the guard wore a woolen hat pulled tight to his ears and he was at least twenty years older than any of the Zionists. All the weight of his face was in his jaw.

Take it out, Aaron said to the others. His voice was a brittle string.

The man came up to the gate and Aaron held out his hands to receive what each Zionist had brought. When they held out their money Hannah saw that she had brought by far the largest amount. She understood now why she had been accepted to this group so quickly. She looked at the stack of worn bills in her hand and thought how different it looked from the fresh, creamy paper her father would bring home from his paper mill. This could become anything, her father would say, cutting the paper and spreading it on the kitchen table, each sheet as crisp as if it stood at attention, waiting for assignment. Thus began one of Hannah's favorite games when she was young. What do you want this paper to be? her father would ask. If she said a book, he would put away the paper and return with a book. If a painting, a painting. What she should have said was: Make it into money. Just give me money, she should have said, each time he asked, until she had gotten from him a roll of bills as thick as her fist.

Instead she had stolen this money, krone by krone, over the space of eleven days. Taken it out of the top left drawer of her father's mahogany desk in small increments, stuffing carefully-cut paper under the top bills to keep the stack at its correct height. She had never stolen from her father before. It was part of being a Zionist. Anyway, what did he need it for? The same stack of bills had sat there undisturbed since the beginning of the war, to provide insulation against an emergency. It had not come, as yet.

Aaron combed the money from their hands, passing first the coins and then the bills through the fence to the man in the woolen hat. The watchman made no pretense of counting it. He dropped the coins in his pants' pocket with a dull clink and turned the stack of bills over once, the way men habitually inspect money that's new to their hand. Then he pushed it deep into his front shirt pocket. He unlocked the gate and waved them in.

They walked quickly down a long driveway, really no more than an alley between factory buildings. On the brick walls there were dashes of white and dark green paint and other colors from years of not-careful-enough drivers. They tried to walk quietly but it was impossible because their shoes kept scuffing against the propaganda pamphlets that covered the ground.

They turned a corner, the watchman in the lead, until they reached a row of trucks. There were several of them, all with large engines and canvas backs. They looked just like the trucks the Germans used to move their soldiers around Denmark and through Copenhagen, the soldiers leaning forward on their forearms and cradling their rifles between their knees. The factory worker adjusted his hat and went around the back of a truck and opened the drawstrings that held together the canvas. Hannah peeked her head in and could see several large wooden boxes.

If this plan worked, Hannah would follow them. In two months she could be in Palestine. Sooner than that even. This factory made parts, machinery for the fast processing of chickens. These trucks brought those parts all the way across Europe. Two of them, Michael and Anise, would hide in one of the trucks, inside a large machine box, until the truck crossed the Turkish border. From there they could tap into known networks, reach Palestine.

Hannah was amazed that a business like this continued during the war. That a truck could drive through Europe uninterrupted, carrying within it a quicker way to pluck chickens. But how was her father's business any different? When she had stolen the money she saw papers on her father's desk, invoices lettered by the vast range of European and Asian alphabets. She didn't want to ask about that, any more than she thought she would ever truly understand how such a thing as a chicken machine business could operate during a world war.

Aaron looked over the truck nervously, pulling on the doors, tapping the tires with his foot, turning his head as if to inspect its underside. The watchman produced a long metal bar from under his coat. He then pried open one of the big boxes in the back of the truck. The rest of them stood there. Anise and the young blond woman held each other just as they had outside the gate: the blond woman crumpled against Anise's chest, Anise looking out vacantly over the crown of her lover's head. Every once in a while

Anise bent her nose to the blond hair. Then she would kiss the woman's head.

Hannah looked at the ground and, in want of something to do, began to read some of the papers that the Germans had dropped in their latest bombing. They were hard to make out in the darkness and no sheet had landed entirely face up. She looked from paper to paper piecing together the message. It described the Germans' successful campaign against the cowardly Russian army. British reports were blatantly false, it said. The Russian campaign was proceeding exactly as planned at the highest levels. A German general would soon be shaking the hand of his Japanese counterpart in a field in the middle of Russia.

It looks ready, Michael said. He climbed into the truck and lowered himself halfway inside the box. All Hannah could see was his chest and head. Aaron came around and stepped onto the rear bumper so he could see inside.

Is it all right? Aaron said.

It's fine.

The watchman motioned toward Anise. Let's go, he said. It was the first thing he had said all evening.

I didn't think it would be so small, Aaron said, to no one in particular.

The blond woman began to cry. Or now Hannah noticed her crying. It was equal parts wetness and noise.

Get it back on? Aaron was saying. He was talking about the lid to the box. It has to look just like before, he said. They're going to look back here.

Don't tell me things I already know, Michael hissed.

Let's go, the watchman said again. Hannah looked at Anise, who looked right back at her for the first time. With a shrug she pushed off the blond woman and climbed into the truck.

At the last moment Aaron handed up to the truck a day's worth of supplies: dried meat, soft potatoes, a lone apple. Then Hannah passed forward a few more bills, to pay the driver to open the box and check on them, give them food and water at isolated points along the road, as long as it took. After the last supplies were handed over the factory worker replaced the lid on the box, pressing down with the flat of his hand for a tight fit. With a screwdriver he pried a small crack in one of the slats for air. Then he drew the flaps of the truck closed.

A few minutes later the three that were left, Hannah, Aaron, and the pretty blond woman, stood outside the factory gate. The blond woman had stopped crying briefly and looked even younger than she did before. She was maybe Hannah's age. This would be a time for compassion, Hannah thought.

I should walk her home, Aaron said to Hannah. I know where she lives. He reached for the woman's arm. She was pliable, watery, and began to walk even before he touched her.

What about me? Hannah thought, but even as she thought it she knew it was a feeling she was expected to have, not one that really belonged to her. She didn't want Aaron's company now and felt that her own thoughts would be burden enough for the long walk back to Bellahøj.

She turned from them as they crossed back over the canal and pursued her own path down a quiet street. A few families had set candles in their second story windows, soft illumination designed to ease them into wakefulness. As Hannah walked she tried to figure how long it would take her to get home and the likelihood she would meet her parents standing in the kitchen. If they were awake, she would be forced to tell them where she had been that night; it would be difficult to lie if she were caught so baldly by her parents in their nightclothes while she still wore yesterday's dress. A part of her felt relieved by this possibility.

In the blue light of the early morning Hannah saw a group of people walking toward her, a strange sound preceding them. She moved to alter her course but found herself all of a sudden brutally tired. As they got closer she realized she was looking at clowns from the amusement park, moving toward her on the narrow street. In the front of their parade an obscenely fat man blew on a tiny trumpet, his cheeks puffing in and out like a bellows. The trumpet emitted no noise. Behind him in single file walked three clowns in half-masque. The masques distorted their faces and swelled their cheekbones and noses like pigs. As they got closer Hannah could see that the outer two walked with a high wire strung between them and the third straddled the wire, stepping in rhythm with the other two, his footsteps brushing the cobblestone. After them walked a man reading from an enormous book; he called out names as if taking attendance or counting prisoners. Behind him followed three men in vastly oversized German uniforms, their heads half-swallowed by the collars, the shoulders bloated.

Every three steps they fumbled their guns in sequence and righted them again. At the very end a disheveled conductor in a flannel tuxedo and stocking feet arced his baton as if leading their steps. As the air-walking clown passed Hannah he shook a cup in her direction and she quickly fumbled in her jacket for coins and dropped them in but they fell through a hole in the cup and rattled to the street. No one paused to pick them up. The parade turned right at the next corner and vanished.

In one month, Hannah thought. In one month I'll fold myself into that box and disappear. She saw herself standing at the glistening shores of Palestine, all odors of past and memory thrown into the sea, a newly scrubbed version of herself inhabiting a new land.

But they only had to wait two weeks for a letter, forwarded through three hands, to report that the two had been discovered ten miles short of the Turkish border. This from a Zionist activist in Turkey who inquired when they failed to appear. The truck driver reported that the Germans had not beaten them or treated them roughly. Instead they brought the two, carrying their possessions, to a nearby train station, destination interior Poland, though why anybody would send Jews there no one could rightly determine.

Part Two

escape

14

the world of birds

For Bakman, notice of martial law arrived by pamphlet, fluttering down out of a grey sky as he left from his shift at Bispebjerg Hospital. It was August; Copenhagen was uniformly hot and damp. He had been back from Gilleleje for a week. In that week, resistance activity had increased notably: there had been seven labor strikes, eleven train bombings, numerous spontaneous rallies in the squares of Copenhagen. To Bakman, Denmark felt like a book being torn apart page by page. And he was a part of it.

Just that morning, on the way to the hospital, he had passed the kiosk where he usually bought his newspaper, now just a blackened and burned shell. The kiosk owner stood over his stand, kicking the ruined boards. The entire inside was sooty as a fireplace. Newspapers the color of coffee grounds scattered through the street.

I sold a newspaper to a German soldier, the owner said to Bakman.

I'm trying to go to work, Bakman said, but the owner, a small man, grabbed him by the sleeve. The owner's clothes smelled pickled, stale, like a man who had smoked a lot of cigarettes in a small space.

Get off of me, Bakman said. The man was wild. Sedation seemed called for.

What was I supposed to do? the man said. I have to eat. I sell newspapers. I sell all kinds. I don't discriminate.

I'm going to be late, Bakman said.

Selling newspapers is my business, the man said. For that someone sets my stand on fire. They dump a bottle of cheap liquor on my newspapers and throw a match. That's all the consideration I get.

People walked by on the other side of the street, staring at Bakman and the owner, who was still holding fast to Bakman's sleeve. I'm not his friend, Bakman wanted to say.

That soldier has been my customer for years, the man said.

I'm sorry, was all Bakman could think to say. He backed away with his hands out. Then he turned and walked quickly to the hospital.

When he arrived he put on his lab coat and descended to the morgue, where he would spend the next eight hours sorting and documenting the unclaimed bodies that arrived from Copenhagen's poor neighborhoods. It was a task he volunteered for as often as possible.

After he had worked for an hour he heard Henrik enter. Bakman knew why he had come. On the blue, silenced chest of a homeless man Bakman sketched out the entire fishing town of Gilleleje. The morgue smelled of chemicals and old shoes. Bakman began at the man's right nipple, placing the fisherman's church there as the main point of reference. He set his metal autopsy scalpels along the sternum and stomach muscles to indicate houses, alleys, the town's lone grocery store. As a final flourish Bakman put the Gilleleje train station down at the navel, so that the train tracks that led to Copenhagen followed the line of hair down to the man's shriveled genitals.

There you have it, Bakman said.

Henrik looked at the temporary town set up on the dead man's chest. He picked his nose absently as he stared at the body.

Bakman knew that he was now a member of the Danish resistance. There was no handshake. No secret induction with men in hoods. No promise of friendship or allegiance, no threat of vengeance for revealing codes. Instead he had passed into this loose arrangement—one that got people arrested or shot or blown apart with homemade bombs—without even knowing when it had happened. Probably at some moment when he was brushing his teeth or eating a piece of stale bread.

Where did you say the sea was? Henrik said, finally.

Bakman pointed to the left nipple, across from the church. Okay then, Henrik said. He reached down and pinched the skin for emphasis. It slacked back into place when he released it. The body had been dead so long it had passed into rigor mortis and back out, moving from soft to hard to soft once again.

Why do you want to know all this? Bakman said.

Henrik shrugged his shoulders as if to say, Who knows? He tapped the dead body on the chest. You're not a handsome man, he said to the body.

What now? Bakman said.

What do you mean?

What do I do now?

You know, Henrik said, grinning at Bakman, I screwed a body down here once.

What?

She was beautiful. Freshly dead. A rich woman, still warm. Not one of your unclaimed friends here. She was wearing pearls and a little black dress. She had died from an aneurysm. There was a little spot of blood on her ear. Just a couple of minutes after I finished her family showed up. Her husband, crying. What do you think? Is she guilty of adultery?

You're lying, Bakman said.

Don't tell me you've never thought about it. Everybody's thought about it.

Bakman waved him off.

Fine, fine, Henrik said. When you're willing to discuss it, you know where to find me. I'm due upstairs.

Henrik exited the morgue. Try not to make too many friends down here, he called to Bakman. Then Bakman heard him whistling in the hallway.

Bakman turned back to his bodies, all set waist-level on the cold, metal tables. Naked, each one. Small events, he thought, pondering the ways each of them had died. Poor gas exchange in the pockets of the lungs. A heart valve suddenly closed. A clot lodged in an artery, a piece of grit in the machine. Liver, kidney, redundant appendix. So many organs, all destined to fail.

Everyone ends up here, he thought, poked and prodded under an unflattering light.

He passed over the bodies, noting identifying marks on his series of charts and forms. Most of these bodies would never be claimed. But it was the nature of his world to keep records, even of things nobody would ever see.

Small events. Someone bends a train track, and delays a supply train. Someone writes an article in an underground newspaper. Someone ignores a German soldier. Someone takes a ride to a fishing town. What did it all add up to? Small events for a small country. He examined the body of a woman, mid-forties, no marks except a scar along her forearm. From what? A kitchen accident? A lover's quarrel? So many questions permanently unanswered. A whole history lost.

When Bakman emerged from the morgue later in the day the street was wet and rain was falling and a new set of pamphlets was billowing from the sky. They covered the street and sat, like wet birds, on the windowsills. Bakman lifted one of the damp pamphlets from the sidewalk. It read: FOR YOUR OWN SAFETY, THE FÜHRER HAS ASSUMED RESPONSIBILITY FOR THE GOVERNANCE OF LOYAL DENMARK. NO LONGER WILL YOU HAVE TO FEAR ACTS OF TERRORISM. THE TRAINS AND STREETS WILL BE SAFE AGAIN.

What does this mean? he thought.

He walked by a café. All the patrons inside had the look of men who were waiting for the morning to become late enough to start drinking beer. They had stopped drinking their coffee and eating their stale pastries and had bent their ears toward a radio propped on the counter. On the radio, a hushed and serious man announced in an upper-class accent that the Danish government had been dissolved; King Christian X was under house arrest at Amalienborg Palace; and that all of Denmark was now under martial law conducted by the German governor. Details to follow.

Is this true? Bakman asked a passerby. The man pulled up his coat and moved away.

Bakman walked quickly in the direction of his tenement apartment. The monkeys have been screeching at night again, and he's been sleeping badly. He still had in his hand the damp pamphlet announcing martial law and he crumpled it and threw it to the ground. Then he noticed a German infantryman standing at the corner. He grabbed the pamphlet for fear of being arrested, either for littering or for insulting the occupation.

This is ridiculous, Bakman thought. I'm a member of the resistance. I'm not afraid of a pamphlet. But what could he do with it? The soldier was standing at the corner, a long-barreled rifle at his shoulder. Here's what I'll do, Bakman thought. I'll throw this pamphlet in his face. Let him clean it up.

But when he reached the German soldier Bakman just stuffed the wet pamphlet back in the pocket of his pants. He walked with his head down past the soldier, who busied himself inspecting his fingernails. As walked farther and farther from the soldier Bakman imagined being arrested, handcuffed and dragged to the police station for the unlawful treatment of a pamphlet. The horrific interrogation that followed, himself stripped and naked in the police basement, blabbering about Gilleleje and the resistance before they had even whipped him with their belts. I gave up everything I knew, he would tell Henrik. Which was nothing.

He reached his apartment, threw off his clothes, put his head down on the bed. The monkeys were screeching from down the block. They screeched and threatened revolt. They demanded to be let out of their cages. Go ahead, Bakman thought. Go ahead and scream. Nobody's listening.

These times are the worst for him, he alone in their small cabin in Gilleleje and Jette gone to Copenhagen. Times like these that Carl is most aware of the indifferent relations between himself and the other fishermen. In Gilleleje each house is a house alone. It seems a natural extension to him, as each fishing boat is alone. The fishermen chat in the harbor, ask about each other's families, trade stories, but when they go out into the water they go alone, each solitary in his boat.

Carl had busied himself for a short time replacing a pane of glass shattered by a bird. This damage to the house had occurred that morning. Carl had seen the entire event while eating his breakfast. He had watched as a small bird, a lark or some such thing, fluttered out from a stand of trees and then hove up by his kitchen window. Its tiny wings scalloped the air, its eyes flicking this way and that, registering, registering. Then it dove into the glass, breaking its own neck and cracking the windowpane.

Carl sat there, amazed at the world of birds. What manner of creature attacked its own reflection? He felt that this event held some lesson for him, though he could not find it in himself to articulate what that was.

He stood outside the house regarding the dead bird on the wet grass where it fell. It displayed no outer sign of injury; it seemed an undamaged bird, albeit one inert and stiff. Carl half-expected it to regain strength, jerk back to life when he nudged it with his boot. It did not. He thought he should dig a small hole and bury it—Jette had a garden spade that would be perfect for the job. But in the end he only pinched the bird by its brittle feet—it was so light—and hurled it in the direction of the compost heap. Lie there now, he thought. Suicidal bird. Later he saw Lucy, their docile retriever, trot by with the bird in her mouth.

Carl then scraped out and replaced the broken pane of glass. He glazed the new glass carefully into its place in the four-pane window until it stood indistinguishable from the others, a quartet of all like panes, and he put the tools and glaze back in the shed. Then he sat down. He had no other tasks real or imagined. He sat some more. He switched on the radio and boiled some coffee. The radio played a Kai Evans tune recorded in Stockholm before the war and Carl wanted to tell Jette that it reminded him of another song he had heard recently on the radio but of course she was not there and he would be speaking to nothing but the blank air of their cottage.

It was, in Denmark, a summer of train accidents. The derailments and explosions engineered by the resistance had built intensity all through the summer months, so that when Carl heard on the radio a new report of crash or injury it no longer held much surprise. Instead he would listen absently to the details of cargo lost or delayed—mostly food from Danish farmers headed to Germany—but since the Germans censored all but the most vague information these reports went by quickly.

All the attacks thus far involved supply trains and all were headed for Germany so the pattern held no mystery. Carl became more interested, though, once Jette began taking the train to Copenhagen.

Carl knew that the resistance would never knowingly target a Danish passenger train but still, Jette was traveling to Copenhagen so often now. He couldn't help but feel that explosions, like an airborne disease, could not be contained. A trigger set on a cargo track might beget some other detonation down on the line to who knew what result and to what point? The thought had been building in him for weeks now. And so yesterday morning, when Jette reminded him that she would be taking the eleven a.m. to Hillerød, with transfer to Copenhagen, he put down his bread and its stingy trace of butter and said simply, No.

No?

No.

Jette looked at him and said, No there is no eleven a.m. to Hillerød or No I will not be found on that train?

No, he repeated, as if it as if were the only worthwhile word in the language and likewise the only one to which he had access.

They were standing in the one bare common room in their cottage, Carl still in his damp fishing clothes and Jette in her next-to-best dress, her standard traveling outfit. When Jette looked at the front door Carl in his heavy boots took two steps to his left, so that he stood in front of it and blocked even the light through the doorway.

Now what are you doing? she asked. Her remark had the tone one might use to scold a mischievous child but there was a hint of something deeper. You really mean to prevent me from leaving?

I do, he said. I don't want you on any trains.

I will not be on *any* trains, she corrected. I will only be on the *one* train that will carry me to my sister's house, where I am expected late this afternoon for dinner.

No, he said.

Are we back to that again? I thought I had married a man with somewhat greater vocabulary.

She looked around her at their tiny house, at the small bedroom where she had slept alone six nights a week for more than twenty years while Carl was fishing in the Sound. She had tried to explain to Carl that leaving for Copenhagen to visit her sister was not the same as leaving him, but this was a distinction he had trouble grasping even before trains began to explode all across Denmark.

I have decided that you should not go, he said. As he said these words he felt all the shame built into his remark and this made him more determined to carry this argument to whatever end it might take. He looked at his wife. She had pleated her blond hair up into a braid and her dress had a collar that ran high up her neck. The braid pulled the skin at her temples tight and gave her something of an angry look.

I am going, she said. It is time for you either to hit me until I am unconscious or get out of the way.

They stood looking at each other, each of them searching for a safe route down from the precipice of that last statement. Jette picked up her bag and walked toward him.

Well? she said.

Carl turned from the doorway. He flinched as Jette pushed past him and walked into the road, carrying the heavy suitcase with both hands. Her train would not leave for more than an hour. All he had accomplished was to lose her company an hour earlier than if he had simply kept quiet.

He had two more days to wait until she would return. Carl looked again at his pane of glass, the sum total of his day's activity. Some pale shavings of glaze remained on the windowsill and beyond that he could see branches working in the wind. Mathiessen replaced Evans on the radio, static and violin in equal measure.

✠ ✠ ✠

Hannah knocked on the door at 32 Nørregade. When Aaron did not answer she waited in his rank and decrepit hallway for a long minute and then knocked again. When he still did not answer she turned the doorknob and it opened for her.

She had hardly seen Aaron in the weeks since the news of the truck disaster, but with the new state of martial law upon the country she felt the need for his guidance, or at least his company.

What she found was a suicide as banal and plain as the factory foreman's had been elegant. A belt slung over an exposed heating pipe, a chair kicked away. His glasses had come off and fallen all the way to the ground and for that reason, if for no other, he no longer looked much like himself. He had left a tin of herring open on the stove and the apartment had already begun to stink. He hadn't been dead very long.

She looked for a note and when she didn't find one she was first angry with him and then simply disappointed. She felt that she deserved one, that it should be addressed to her by name and that he should tell her all the things he was thinking before he killed himself. She found none. She thought she should try to pull him down but couldn't figure a way to do that that preserved either his dignity or her own. So she left him in the bedroom and closed the door behind her.

She could not call the police, that was plain. She could think of no way to involve them that would not end with her being questioned, probably in front of her parents. Likewise she had no phone number and no address for any of the other Zionists. She searched the apartment again but found no letters from Aaron's family, no photos, nothing that suggested he had any relatives that might feel the obligation to receive this particular news. Aside from his books and pamphlets she found only one slip of paper with a Copenhagen phone number. It had the letter *H* written above it. When she dialed the number the operator at Bispebjerg Hospital answered and she soon found herself talking to a man named Henrik.

15

creatures heading for extinction

Suddenly his life had become about Jews. Bakman was carrying a urine sample to the lab when Henrik grabbed him and shoved him into a janitor's closet. He pushed Bakman into the mops and broom handles like a lover seeking a warm, dry place.

You're in this, Henrik said. Now you're going to have to do your part.

The Germans would not be satisfied just with martial law, Henrik whispered. The Danish government had been dissolved, yes. The Germans had arrested Communists, trade unionists, actors. But the strikes and the protests had continued. But it hadn't stopped the strikes and the protests, the counter-leaflets, the smuggling of explosives. Would they arrest the whole country?

No, Henrik said. The German needs something else. He has a rotting tooth and it needs to be pulled.

What are you talking about? Bakman said.

The Jews, Henrik answered.

They heard steps in the hospital hallway. The clip-clop of nurses' shoes, two people, maybe three. Henrik pressed closer to Bakman. Something poked Bakman in the thigh.

Don't you see? Henrik said. They're going to take the Jews. Pack them up and drive them away. It's what the Germans do. They take them and they turn them into ashes. They grind them into wallpaper paste.

How do you know? Bakman said. His voice was loud in the small closet. He could feel Henrik's breath against his cheek. He also wanted to ask, Why are we in this stupid closet? But this was how Henrik needed it to be. It was just like elementary school. Big, bossy Henrik always got to be the hero, while he made Bakman impersonate a variety of villains—pirate, invader, evil scientist—whose schemes would come unraveled. More than once it ended with Henrik yanking Bakman's pants down in front of their schoolmates.

Everybody knows, Henrik said. People don't just disappear, Bakman. They disappear to *somewhere.* There's no mystery. It's just that some people—he tapped Bakman on the chest—don't want to see what's going on.

I really don't want a philosophy lecture in a closet, Bakman said. A broom handle was jabbing into his back.

Just be ready, Henrik said.

For what? Bakman answered. But Henrik was already halfway out the closet door. He peeked to see if anyone was looking, then ducked out the door, leaving Bakman alone in the dark to fumble among the mops and buckets.

Henrik was right about one thing, Bakman thought—the Germans did spend a lot of time talking about Jews. They ran movies and radio broadcasts, put up advertising posters highlighting every negative feature of that particular race. The movies, Bakman felt, lacked good plots and were poorly acted.

Bakman stumbled out of the closet, adjusting his glasses, blinking at the harsh light of the hallway. He felt like a nervous rodent edging out of a hole. Two young nurses stood in the hallway, giggling at the sight of him coming of the janitor's closet with a urine sample in his hand. Bakman recognized them from the geriatric ward on the hospital's top floor. It was the most gossipy department, he noted with some regret—the nurses spent all day discussing their co-workers over the heads of their deaf and senile patients.

What? Bakman said to them. They turned to each other and whispered again. Then they walked away.

Stupid Henrik and his stupid resistance, Bakman thought. It's just making me look bad.

Bakman didn't understand this fascination with Jews. As far as Bakman was concerned there was no such thing as a Jew, not like the Germans claimed, at least not here in Denmark. And if there was such a thing in other countries he, Bakman, had no way of knowing it, never having had the privilege of leaving this tiny sea-squashed country for the purpose of seeing Jews or any other purpose whatsoever. Perhaps there did exist Jews in other countries. Perhaps in other countries they kept these Jews rounded up in particular cages like the animals in the zoo next to Bakman's flat, the ones he could hear screeching at night and begging to be let go. Perhaps like the monkeys these Jews spit and threw feces at the people who came to watch them, these people who, after all, just wanted to observe them, just wanted to have a chance to look at them and appreciate them from a safe, sterilized distance.

Maybe this was all the Germans wanted, despite all the noise about invasions and occupations and exterminations: to be the zookeepers of Europe. To separate the Swedes and the Danes and the Czechs and the Poles into their respective cages where they could no longer harm each other as they were prone to do in their natural habitats. And after that the Africans and the Asians and the various species of the Americas, each divided and kept in sufficient food and water by the German, who was of course known throughout Europe for his taxonomic rigor and his devotion to scientific inquiry.

It all made a certain amount of sense to Bakman, who was a scientific man, though not an educated one. His father had been an educated man, had spoken Swedish, German, French and English in addition to Danish and had studied the newspaper for exactly one half-hour every morning and who had died at the age of forty-two from what was in truth nothing more than a muscular cough, leaving Bakman in the care of a strict and bitter grandmother who had herself expired soon enough, sitting up in her hard-backed chair in front of a second-floor window, shouting harsh and deprecating remarks to passersby on the street below up to her final throaty breath, leaving Bakman this time in no one's care but his own, through which he had persevered and studied and even achieved a respectable profession, a profession he had reached by keeping his nose to the grindstone and his head down and his chin up and by eliminating all matters not to the point like attending football matches and saving Jews. And now this was exactly what Henrik wanted him to do. When for all he knew it was an act of mercy on the Germans' part. For hadn't he heard his whole life and even the few times he had been in church that the Jew was a dying and redundant race, and perhaps all the Germans wanted after all was to set up their little zoo, and what is the purpose of a zoo but the safety and preservation of those creatures headed for extinction?

If you put it in those terms, Bakman thought, it made a certain amount of sense, not just the occupation but the entire war. But were those the right terms? How was a person to know?

Bakman gave the urine sample to a scowling lab worker and signed out of the hospital. He decided to walk around Copenhagen. He wanted to see his city. Some air, he thought. That's what I need to clear my head.

As soon as he turned onto the leafy street in front of the hospital, though, he realized that he wasn't, in fact, about to embark on a leisurely tour of Copenhagen. Instead, he was already moving like a miser down the street that led directly back to his tiny room in Nørrebro. His body was like an appendage, a stalk attached to an over-busy brain, and all of its functions cleaved toward the autonomic. Even locomotion was beyond his conscious control. It had joined with breathing and digestion, all of them falling together into the broad category of involuntary behaviors.

Bakman walked across the Østerbrogade, the bridge over the canal that formed the southernmost end of his Nørrebro neighborhood. A single sheet of newspaper floated in grey, still water. It twirled slowly, a rudderless boat adrift in the canal. Looking at the water made Bakman think once again of Nyhaven, the neighborhood at the other end of the city, with the fishing boats and the café he had frequented at the beginning of the summer. In his memory it was all so much friendlier and warmer, the coffee richer, the waitress pretty and flirting. He felt a longing for the unemployed fishermen there, though he had not once spoken to any of them, and for the café owner and his small welcomes. Though it was mere months ago, it felt like stacks of years.

He didn't even know why he had stopped going there. It seemed, back then, that he was about to embark on an important time in his life. Instead he had spent the summer mostly in the morgue. He would have to buckle down, not spend so much time idling.

He continued into Nørrebro. The streets were empty even though it was the middle of the day. Where is everybody hiding? he thought. One sharp look from the Germans and this is what you do? The cafés were like abandoned caves; even the waiters were gone. It was a warm summer day in Copenhagen: the sidewalks should have been spilling over with pedestrians and shoppers. He hated that he could walk the street without adjusting for others' walking paths, without corkscrewing his body around the café sitters and their chairs, their jutting elbows, their gestures. He sought impediment, stirred angry at its absence.

The high-level doctors at the hospital—the ones who made up Henrik's resistance group—didn't even know his name. It figured that Henrik would trust him with something inconsequential—like Jews being deported—while keeping all the really important information to himself.

As soon as Henrik finishes his shift, Bakman thought, he's going to hear it from me. He really is. I'll show him what a serious person I am. Bakman continued on toward the sullen façade of his building.

As soon as he climbed the stairs to his apartment he tripped over a washing bucket that had been left in the hallway and draped with rags. The water sloshed up and soaked his pant leg from knee to foot.

Shit, he said. He proceeded to his room stomping the wet leg to shake off the water. He looked like a man possessed by a spirit, a malevolent ghost. Water collected between sock and undersole. He stomped again.

From Henrik's apartment next door he heard the foreign cleaning woman, Mrs. Krebnow. The floorboards creaked under her heavy legs. Stupid bitch. Leaving her bucket in the hallway.

He opened the door to his apartment. The woman's cleaning had always been lousy. But the last few weeks had been worse than usual.

It was as if she were taking an agricultural approach to cleaning his tiny apartment, doing certain sections each week while leaving others to lie fallow. She scrubbed his kitchen counter, but left dishes to fester in the sink. She treated his bed with disdain, refused to touch it.

He took off the wet shoe and wet sock. Dug through his laundry only to find that she had somehow removed all his socks, clean and dirty both. He could not find any. He was standing there with one bare foot and a shoe in his right hand when he saw the woman waddle by the hallway door.

Get in here, he said.

She stopped in the hallway holding a rag in one hand. She had poor eyesight and looked into the apartment as if trying to perceive something at a great distance. She squinted at him.

I said get in here.

She said something back to him in Polish, maybe Yiddish.

I don't speak that language, he said. Don't speak it to me.

She shrugged her shoulders and began to walk away. Just like Henrik would do. Bakman strode after her in a one-shoed limp, grabbed her by the arm. He pulled her down the hallway. She pulled against him.

I said, get in here! he repeated.

She yelled back at him, her words all harsh vowels and staccato consonants. He pulled her up to his worn kitchen table and sent all the books and dirty plates she had left there flying with a swipe of his arm. A plate broke against the floor. She was a heavy woman. He pushed her against the table until he had her hand and her rag pressed to the tabletop.

Clean, he said. Clean.

He pushed her face toward the table with one hand and with the other forced her to clean in a circular motion. The old woman began to sob. Bakman pushed harder. Finally she pulled loose from him in a spasm of arms and Slavic intonations. She threw the rag at him. Bakman ducked it, but his bare foot slipped on the broken plate and he landed on his ass.

Why should I try to save you, he yelled. Why! Why!

The woman scurried from the apartment. She was crying in great heaves.

I don't care if they pack you away in a truck, he yelled. I hope they do! I hope they do! He ran to the door but she had already clomped away down the stairs.

I'm not helping! he said to the empty hallway. Just you wait! I don't care what Henrik says. I'm not helping any of you! Why should I!

Then she was gone. He returned to his apartment, looked at the mess on the floor. Stupid resistance, he thought.

16

the busy Jerusalem streets

The apartment where Jette stayed with her sister, brother-in-law, and their three children in working-class Christianshavn was a cramped sequence of box-like rooms, water-stained ceilings, and mice that darted across the floor at regular hours. Their washtub sat right next to the stove. There was a communal water closet in the building's hallway with a door that did not fully shut.

Jette shared a bed with the thirteen-year-old daughter and the two sons, ten and twelve years, slept in the next bed, separated from Jette and the girl by a hanging curtain. Jette could hear them jerking off at night under the covers and one morning while changing her clothes she looked up to see them staring at her through the thin divider, each boy with his hand in his underwear.

The first morning of her visit she walked across the Knipples Bridge and into the center of Copenhagen. She strolled with great interest past the shops of the Strøget amongst the other Copenhagen women. There was much to see, even in the midst of this war. She walked to Amalienborg Palace where the royal gardener trimmed azaleas, tulips, and cornflowers under the watchful eye of German soldiers. In the afternoon she wandered into Kongens Have Park to watch a puppeteer work a show that only occasionally referred to the German occupation.

Nobody knew her here, knew what kind of woman she was. She told another woman in Kongens Have that she was the mother of three children under ten—a handful, yes, but such a blessing, weren't they? and she couldn't wait to see them again, except that their father had taken them to lunch, just to give her some time alone. Later she declared herself a grandmother, shopping along the Strøget for something adorable for the latest addition to her wide, bountiful family, and would the salesgirl help choose something of a medium price? In Copenhagen she was not barren, if she did not want to be. Nobody would know. She could say anything in this busy city, invent whole reams of children, using a detail from her niece or nephews and adding the name of a dead relative or particular ability in sports or mathematics. None of the people she spoke to knew any different. In Gilleleje, the other wives resented her prettiness and pitied her inability to produce for Carl a son, both in equal measure.

She came home, gave her niece the cheap necklace she had bought at the store along the Strøget. She had used up most of her and Carl's money on the train fare, had only enough for the trip back to Gilleleje. There was no room for generosity in her sister's meager household. That night they listened to the radio describe the edicts of martial law. Outside Germans patrolled the streets of Christianshavn, manned their checkpoints on each bridge, poked through bags and handpurses for any evidence of the Danish resistance.

And what about Carl? Jette woke up early that second night thinking about him. She sat on the bed that she shared with her niece, watched the girl shuffle and roll over. The niece was plump, and she slept like a satisfied cat, curled into the corner, her face hidden behind her arm. It was not even five o'clock in the morning. The sun had begun to throw dirty light onto the streets. In Gilleleje, Carl would be coming home bearing his half-empty nets.

He had given up so easily. After each of Jette's miscarriages Carl had tied up the bloody sheets and set them aside to wash. He saved nothing, didn't want to name the still gender-less child or claim a portion of the graveyard outside the fishermen's church. The third time she had miscarried, just a year before, she was standing in the yard and she bled out from under her dress into the dirt. Later that afternoon as she lay resting on their bed, she looked through the window and saw him in the yard with a shovel, turning dirt over the dark spot. The blood and more viscous matter had already soaked into the dirt and he worked it over twice and then patted it with the back of the shovel. Then he came inside and washed his hands and set to boiling water for coffee.

What she had wanted to say to him. That they would go on and build a life and not be satisfied with an empty house and long nights with him gone on the Sound. But she had not said that. Instead she had waited for him to come in bearing two mugs of black coffee and held him and drank the coffee and stroked his hair as if he, not she, were the one needing solace and consolation.

Jette left the bed where her niece was sleeping. She met her sister, bleary-eyed and blinking, in the hallway.

What's the matter? the sister said.

Nothing.

I thought it was one of the kids, the sister said.

She padded back to her own room.

Jette walked quietly to her sister's small kitchen and began frying an egg. There was little butter in the icebox and so she used it sparingly, working the spatula along the edges of the egg to keep it from sticking. By the time the egg was hard Jette realized she was crying. She cut into the egg yolk with a fork and the yellow liquid seeped out to the far edges of the pan like a schoolbook map of an expanding empire. She ate the egg straight out of the pan in small bites and in between bringing the wet slices to her mouth she wiped her eyes with the foresleeve of her nightgown.

After a while the sun rose full on Christianshavn and through the window she saw a couple stagger from their house, blinking and still fighting off sleep. They moved mechanically, as if learning the process of walking with each new step. A lone German truck rattled down the street. Jette's two nephews woke and argued about who would have first use of the toilet. They rushed through the house, bumping Jette at the stove, and wrestled at the front door. Then they chased each other down the hallway to the water closet.

✣ ✣ ✣

In her room upstairs at Bellahøj, Hannah dresses herself for Rosh Hashanah evening, applying in precise order the undergarments, the stockings, the camisole, and finally over all that the dress itself, a complicated length of ivory-colored marocain with rows of matching ivory silk fringe running down its front in delicate lines. Her hair she ties with a ribbon, silk, blue.

Last night she had cried over Aaron Marcus. Not because she loved him. He was argumentative, spiteful, often pathetic. He dominated conversations with dubious political theories. He had bad breath.

Still, she had cried. She had mortgaged everything for this dream of Jerusalem and Palestine and now all she had left was her life in Copenhagen. Months of work, gone. She had declined to make any friends at the university and as soon as this semester ended her parents would receive a letter sketching out her long absence from classes and detailing in polite sentences the terms of her expulsion. She had no marriage prospects. With Aaron's death, the Zionist group had completely disintegrated. She sits on her bed in her extravagant, stiff dress and realizes once again as she did last night what a foolish and embarrassing enterprise it had been the whole time. She is nineteen years old and four months is a very long time to have spent on anything.

She has no one she can tell about this. No aunt, no sisterly cousin, no one. She had cried quietly, pressing her face into her pillow so that, to someone outside the room, it might have sounded only like simple breathing. She had cried for over an hour and the whole time she could hear her parents walking through the house performing their evening tasks. She would not call out to them. They were her parents, yes, but they felt like some strange presence come to occupy the house, two guards left behind to represent an entire force of misunderstanding and distance.

In the morning she left the house early. Her father was already gone to work and her mother remained in her bedroom under the stupor of her latest headache remedy. The only one awake in the house was the maid, who stood in the kitchen slicing carrots for Rosh Hashanah dinner. She had already chopped onions and the pieces sat curved and glistening in a bowl on the counter.

Hannah wanted to walk across the city, all the way to Christianshavn. She wanted to find the man in the fisherman's sweater. She had spent a total of three occasions in his company; each time he had been wordless and odd. He would sit in his alley in total silence, an attitude that always prompted Hannah to speak, if only to fill the void. She didn't know what she might say today, except that the sound of her own voice against that silent background might be comforting.

She left her house and walked through the streets of Copenhagen. All the doorways, windows, and row houses she passed seemed to taunt her with the undeniable fact that they were not Jerusalem. She passed newsstands and cigarette kiosks and their racks stood half empty because so many papers had been shuttered by the martial government. One newsvendor stood in front of a tiny booth sprucing old flowers, trying to make his remaining newspapers pass for abundance. He had little to work with, though, so he opened up one newspaper with a surgeon's care, spreading its sections side by side on his countertop as if each were an independent volume and could be sold for its own kroner.

She continued through the city. She walked past Slotsholmen, where the ornate buildings held the shell of a Danish government that no longer really existed. What few government men who still had positions had stayed home out of protest and she encountered only a single cleaning worker in the entire vast courtyard. She passed the Royal Library, where a few determined scholars entered the doors, bent like penitents under the loads of their heavy volumes.

She crossed the Knipples Bridge into Christianshavn. She walked by a corner pub with its door thrown open in an attempt to freshen the air. Inside, a few haggard drinkers had either stayed very late or arrived very early. One man at the bar tipped his glass to her as she passed. She walked faster.

She moved deeper into Christianshavn, looking for the street that would lead her to the next street and finally into his alleyway. She could not find it.

What an idiot, she thought. How do I expect to reach Jerusalem when I can't even find a simple street in

Copenhagen? But something was amiss. These were the streets she had been on before. Where were all the people? She passed empty storefronts, abandoned carts of goods. Laundry hung in an alleyway.

I am walking in circles, she thought. She had been gone from her house for hours. She thought of the maid happily slicing carrots and she wished only to be back in her house in Bellahøj.

She walked down another street. Where was everyone? Empty windows, barren sidewalks. She worked her way down the broken storefronts until she found what she thought was his alley. Nothing. Just a few papers scattered on the ground, a derelict dresser he had been burning drawer-by-drawer, empty tins of food. But he was not there.

She backed away from the alley. She saw a young boy, maybe six years old, staring at her from a second-story window. His face was dirty and his chest was bare. What happened here? Hannah called to him. But when he saw her the boy shied away from the window and shut it behind him.

I cannot stay here any longer, she thought. She hurried back across the Knipples Bridge to central Copenhagen. She was exhausted, morose, hungry. The first store she found open was a small butcher shop. It was worn and dingy and its offerings ran to the lesser parts of meat, suet, silverskin, boiled hooves, viscera. There was no one behind the counter. The glass case was moist from condensation and she put her hand out to test the glass. It was cold. She curled her arms like a pillow and put her head down against the glass. An old man emerged from a back room, wiping blood and sinews on his apron.

Are you all right? he asked.

I'm tired, was all she could say.

Two German officers entered the shop. They wore black uniforms with collars buttoned all the way to their necks and they filled the shop with the smell of gun oil. One officer was wiping his pistol with a rag and he looked into the case and then tapped on the glass with the pistol barrel to indicate the meats he wanted. Hannah lifted her head from the counter and moved slowly away from it. Then she slank past them into the street.

When she finally reached home the maid had finished for the day, and sliced, chopped, and minced vegetables sat in plates and bowls on the counter and on the kitchen table. Her father had come home early from work as he always did before a holiday and now stood in the kitchen as if trying to predict what sort of Rosh Hashanah dinner he might reasonably expect from such disparate parts. As soon as he saw Hannah his face grew dark.

Where have you been? he said.

Out for a walk.

She crossed through kitchen toward the stairs. Her father grabbed her wrist, stopping her short.

That won't do, he said.

What?

Your behavior is unacceptable. You think I don't know what you've been up to?

What are you talking about?

I used favors to get you into the university. You think favors are easy to come by these days?

I didn't ask you to, Hannah said. She tried to pull her arm free. Her father heard her mother coming down the stairs and let go of Hannah's arm.

Behave yourself, he said.

Her mother appeared at the bottom of the stairs, dazed and wild-looking. What's going on here? she said. She was still in her nightgown and her hair was everywhere.

This isn't over, Bergstrom hissed. Hannah passed her mother and went up the stairs.

An hour later her mother knocked on her door. She was carrying the ivory dress and she herself had undergone a type of transformation, her hair perfectly styled, the nightgown gone, and in its place a silk dress that swept along the floor when she walked.

What's that for? Hannah said, looking at the dress her mother held draped over her arm. Its long skirt fanned and floated just a few inches over the floor.

It's time to go to *shul.* Your father's waiting.

So?

It's Rosh Hashanah. Your father likes to show you off.

There's nothing to show off.

You let him decide that.

What about you?

I have things to do here, her mother said. Her mother normally had little use for the details of cooking but took great pride and interest in the presentation of the Jewish holidays, spending hours arranging the china, serving dishes, silverware, *Kiddush* cup, and candlesticks, to choosing the linens and the wine, and to eyeing with suspicion the maid's preparations of the food. She liked to perform these tasks while Hannah and her father were away at synagogue, so that when they returned she could present the lavish table to them, accepting no compliments but gazing at her extravagant work with obvious satisfaction.

Your father makes sacrifices for you, her mother remarked. We both do.

Hannah said nothing but accepted the dress. She sat there with her arms crossed until her mother left the room. When Hannah put the dress on, she marveled that her mother—who spent one day of every four entirely confined to her bed and made little effort to engage Hannah in conversation—had observed her daughter so closely that she could select and alter a dress that corresponded so perfectly to her dimensions. It fit Hannah as if she herself had been the tailor's dummy. It was a beautiful dress, its texture like the coat of some pampered animal. She had just put it on when she heard a violent knocking at the front door of the house.

Hannah looked out her window to see Bothke, her friend Mari's father, banging wildly on their door. He was wearing his Danish Nazi uniform. Hannah ran downstairs to her parents.

Bergstrom! Bothke yelled.

Hannah's father and mother hurried to the door. They looked at each other.

Bergstrom! Bothke yelled again.

What do you want?

Let me in! I need to talk to you!

Bergstrom looked out the window. Bothke was alone; the rest of street was empty. The other big houses had their lights on. He looked next door to Bothke's house, the smallest on the block. He could see Bothke's wife hunched over the sink in their kitchen.

Bergstrom opened the door and Bothke stormed in. The collar of his brownshirt uniform was torn away. The swastika pin hung on a ripped tangle of threads. His face was red and on the left side there were four welts in the shape of fingers or a leather glove.

What do want, Bothke? Bergstrom demanded. We're busy.

I know about your holiday, Bothke spat. I need to talk to you.

Bergstrom looked at his wife and then at Hannah. Fine, he said to Bothke. Bergstrom walked him to the parlor, and Hannah and her mother had no choice but follow. Bothke sat down in Bergstrom's reading chair and threw his arm on the fancy marquetry table that stood next to it. Bergstrom's thick *History of Scandinavia* lay open where he had been reading it. No one else sat down. Her mother remained in the archway, the French doors open behind her. She kept her hand on the telephone.

Get on with it, Bergstrom said.

You have anything to drink around here?

Fine, Bergstrom said. He looked at his wife. Get him something to drink.

Hannah's mother brought the bottle of Peter Heering she had set aside for after dinner. She set it on the marquetry table along with a water glass. Bothke looked at the bottle dubiously. Then he unscrewed the cap and tipped a heavy shot into the glass. Cherry liquor skipped off the glass rim and pooled in drops on the glazed tabletop.

Get on with it, Bothke, Bergstrom said again. You're trying my patience.

They're sending you to Poland, Bothke announced, then drank some of the Peter Heering.

Who's sending me to Poland? Bergstrom said.

Who. The Germans. Who do you think?

They all stood there, saying nothing. You're being ridiculous, Bergstrom said finally. Hannah, he said, call next door. Tell his wife to come bring him home.

You think I don't know what's going to happen? Bothke said. You think I don't know? I was there. At 14 Læderstræde. I heard them talking. I speak German, you know.

Go back to your fascist meeting. Leave us alone.

Fuck the Germans! Bothke said. Fuck them.

Bothke told them that he had gone to 14 Læderstræde that morning, just as he had several times over the summer to try to get information, any information, about his son's posting. Usually the liaison had claimed that it was exceptionally difficult to get solid information about the Russian front. But he would promise to investigate the status of the S.S. unit to which the younger Bothke had been assigned and contact the family as soon as he received a report.

This morning, though, it had been different. There were soldiers everywhere. The German headquarters was full, busy as a train station. Bothke approached the front desk. The clerk was gone, replaced by a big sergeant with infantry medals on his uniform.

Where's the day clerk? Bothke said.

He's been sent back to Germany, the sergeant replied, in a thick Bavarian accent.

I need to know about my son, Bothke said. He's fighting for the glory of Germany and Denmark, and . . .

Stop. Stop right there. I don't have time for this.

What do you mean you don't have time? I am a fully inducted member of the Danish National Socialist Party. I hold the rank of Commander.

I don't care if you're a member of the Copenhagen Marching Band, the sergeant said. I don't have time for you. We've got real business here. We've been wasting time in this country long enough.

The sergeant looked back at the papers on his desk. Bothke put his hand down on the papers. I need to know about my son, he said.

Now you're going to shut up, the sergeant said. He came around the desk.

Stay away from me, Bothke said. I just want to know about my son.

You sound like a woman. Do you know how many families in Germany are waiting for information about their sons?

We're all fighting for the same Fatherland.

You Danish prick. You're not fighting for anything. You're coming in here and taking up valuable time when we're trying to plan a very important operation.

Stay away from me, Bothke said again.

You look like a Jew, the sergeant said. Do you think he's a Jew? he said to the other soldiers.

I'm not a Jew. I have my Aryan documentation. It shows a three hundred year bloodline.

Bothke pulled a folded piece of paper from his breast pocket, held it out with two shaking fingers. One of the other soldiers took it.

Jews know how to get those papers, the sergeant said. He took hold of Bothke by the face, squeezed. Then he shoved him against the wall. There was a bulletin board with pins and they pressed into the back of Bothke's head.

Let him go, the other soldier said.

Not yet.

Let him go, the other soldier repeated.

Sure, the sergeant said. Better go home, the sergeant told Bothke. Before I come to your house and show your wife what a real uniform looks like.

Why haven't we heard anything about this? Hannah asked Bothke.

Be quiet, Hannah, her father said.

Bothke put his hand on his glass of cherry liquor. They've always been planning to round up the Jews, Bothke said. You're lucky you lasted this long.

You need to leave, Bergstrom said.

Fine. Fine. But you'll see. Soon enough.

You need to leave now.

Fuck all of you, Bothke said as he walked out the door. He tried to button his collar but the torn hem wouldn't take.

✣ ✣ ✣

That same evening, the third day of her visit, the 30th of September 1943, Jette boarded the train back to Gilleleje. There were no Jews that she could see, not yet.

That afternoon Jette's brother-in-law had come home bearing a rumor he had heard at Bispebjerg Hospital, where he had gone after giving himself a bad cut in his shop. The young doctor who sutured his wound asked him if he had a truck that might be hired. I need to arrange transport, the doctor said.

For who?

For Jews.

Of course he had no truck, he told Jette. If he did, he would not waste it on Jews. He balled and opened his injured hand, tested the stitches with his finger.

Excuse me, Jette said. Then she ran off to her room.

She gathered her few remaining kroner, packed her floral-patterned suitcase, hurried a goodbye to her sister and the children. She boarded a train back to Gilleleje, moving past the farmhouses and wide fields. Copenhagen was already receding in her mind like a forgotten language.

She will have a child now. She knows it. She just has to be in Gilleleje to receive it. The train is empty—who travels to the countryside in the middle of the afternoon, in a country under martial law?—but soon there would be many people fleeing the Germans, if her brother-in-law is to be believed.

She is a fisherman's wife. She knows how hard it is to cross the water. It is difficult enough to take a baby on a car ride—never mind on a rickety boat across the Sound. Or there might not be enough boats. Or a storm might come. There are so many ways it could go wrong.

She will go to Gilleleje and wait for the Jews to come. And when they do, she will say to one of them: give me your child. If they catch you, your child will still be safe. You could drown or get shot or travel all the way to Sweden just to be sent back. Then what would happen to your baby? She will say it plainly to these Jews, so they understand the risks. Then they will see the value of giving their child to her.

Jette looks at all the empty seats around her. She hasn't seen the ticket-taker since he walked through the car an hour earlier. Her train seat is brown, the color of dried leaves, and its upholstery has split open like an old mattress. She will raise the baby as a Jew, she thinks, because that will be important to the parents and she does not want to lie. She doesn't know anything about being a Jew, but she will ask the pastor, who has no doubt read about Jews in his books. When the Germans arrived three years ago they put up posters with the Danish proverb: *Where there is room in the heart, there is room in the house.* And she has so much room in her heart.

The Faeroe Islander had spent the previous night at the bombed factory of Burmeister & Wein, the vast shipbuilding business at the edge of Christianshavn. Two years earlier the factory had begun the profitable business of building U-Boat engines and seven months after that it had been destroyed by the ten conscripted members of a British Lancaster, which dropped a stack of bombs out of a bright and flakless sky, leveling one end of the factory and killing twenty-two Danish workers. Since then it lay empty. The Faeroese came here regularly for scavenged parts with which to furnish his alley and to wander among the broken machines of the factory floor, where a security guard patrolled indifferently or failed to come to work for days at a time.

He entered the factory through a side door and walked by the dusty drill presses and welding tanks, some covered with drop cloths and others left exposed and rusting under the holes in the roof. He fingered the abandoned wrenches, tap hammers, measuring calipers. A full moon shone like a clock face through the long factory windows, casting a pale illumination on the dead machines. He shook an old tarp to test it for its integrity and dust motes scattered up and flitted in the moonlight.

He walked to the desk at the front where the absent guard had left his set of skeleton keys and the wrappings of a sandwich. He opened the guard's logbook and flipped through the scant markings and blank entries. Toward the end of the book the guard had drawn a simple *Life of Jesus* and the Faeroe Islander looked on as the baby King was born, performed miracles, and died in the busy Jerusalem streets. On the last page he floated to heaven on shafts of light. The Faeroe Islander closed the book and continued on his way through the factory.

On a window ledge he found a nest constructed of newspaper and a generous amount of sawdust. In it a bird had left a batch of yellow, speckled, and very tiny eggs, each the size of the top joint of his thumb. He selected one and cracked it open with his fingernail and sucked the yolk and clingy white through the hole in the shell. The others he left there. In the nest the parent bird had placed the end of a sharp carving hammer, the wooden handle broken off and splintered in its eye. This he put in his pocket.

When he finally left the factory it was early morning and a fog was rising off the streets and hanging on the roofs of the houses. An old woman carried a dirty sheet full of laundry and they walked near each other down the streets of Christianshavn like companions, but when she turned down an alleyway, shifting her load to help with the turn, he did not follow and instead walked on toward the voluntary ghetto.

When he reached his alleyway the Germans were already on the street, calling families out of their houses and comparing them to lists they kept on clipboards and measuring the people against documented facts of birth, gender, and country of origin. He discovered in his pocket the remains of the factory guard's sandwich and this he ate from the safety of his alleyway as one large German grabbed up a street vendor and held him closely by the head as if to inspect his teeth. The man had been selling coal and another German pulled little blackened squares from the man's pocket and dumped them on the sidewalk. Finally they threw him down with his wares and he gathered the pieces of coal up again in his sooty lap. Two boys ran from the line of people and took off down the narrow street. The soldier chased them for a moment and then stopped and unhooked his rifle and fired it in the air after them. The shot made a terrible report and one woman held her hands over her ears until long after the shot had dissipated. Then the other soldiers waved to the German who had fired his rifle and they all stepped back into their truck and drove away. The Faeroe Islander threw the paper wrappings of the sandwich into the street and the sellers pulled their carts from their alleyways into their normal positions and the coal seller auctioned his stock at inflated prices since he himself was now an object of some interest and fascination.

The Faeroe Islander climbed back into his alley and began to wait for the girl. He did not know if she would come. In the afternoon a brief rain fell and he climbed under the curved shelter he had built and watched the water drip off the boards in front of him. With the clawed end of the broken carving hammer he cleaned the soles of his boots, digging in the worn grooves and cleaning the grit from the hammer by tapping it against the brick wall next to him. Later someone in the building above him began to cook a greasy stew and with the rain still dripping he thought of wet sheep. Still she did not come. He waited.

An hour later the Germans returned again, this time with three trucks full with soldiers and rifles. They flashed through the ghetto like water through a narrow channel, driving the inhabitants before them. They beat vendors and shop owners and passersby and old men out of chance or indifference. With their lists and clipboards they identified those that corresponded to their understanding of Jewish names and those they hit with their rifles and gathered into their trucks and the others they let vanish among the hanging laundry and boarded-up windows. The Faeroe Islander had been sleeping in his alley and when he woke the street in front of him was empty. Even the carts were gone. There was no movement in the boarded-up storefronts and the windows above were slack and empty. He began to walk.

17

a desolate and oily sea

Bakman woke to deep regret. His bullying was in evidence all through the apartment: books on the floor, a damp rag hung on a chair. If he could find Mrs. Krebnow, he could apologize, possibly even undo his actions of the previous day. It was as simple as that. But where to look? He had no idea where this cleaning woman lived, where she might have fled to.

I may not know anything about the resistance, he thought, but I know Copenhagen. This is my city. He decided he would cross Copenhagen until he found her.

He left his apartment and headed toward the center of the city. He would go neighborhood-by-neighborhood, door-to-door if he had to.

He walked past the Royal Stock Exchange with its vain dragon spire atop, past the miniature Poseidons, water nymphs, curved whales, carved in tiny arrangements on door faces, arches and cornices. He walked through a square, renowned in the prewar years for its lunchtime street performers, now the site of a weapons collection. As he crossed the square Bakman passed a great pyramid of impounded weaponry, turned over by the citizens of Copenhagen to their German overseers as per martial law. The pile, already to the height of Bakman's shoulders, included hunting rifles and wooden-handled pistols; knives of every length and variety; an antique crossbow; a hooked machete from the Indian subcontinent; a dueling pistol that had killed in turn the men 256th, 112th, and 14th in line to the throne of Luxembourg; and a serrated knife with a left-handed grip that had figured in a series of spectacular Copenhagen killings in the 1920's. Each of these weapons as added was marked and described by a Danish policeman supervised by a German lieutenant. Bakman passed close enough to smell a German soldier's cologne and to hear the faint sobbing of a man turning over the pistol with which his son had committed suicide. A line extended down the sidewalk as citizens waited to add their possessions to the catalogue.

At the corner Bakman arrived at Anneborg street, where a left turn would take him down toward the zoo and back to his tenement apartment. He turned right instead. He had never felt the war so presently as today. Each moment of the war until this day had been only a small adjustment: cold water instead of lukewarm in his shower, ersatz coffee instead of real, and milk only on occasion. A small stockpiling of incident. A discontinuity of small things. But today—seeing the mound of small weaponry at a fashionable square—Bakman knows that something vital has changed, feels the longing in his stomach that exists now or has existed always but he only now acknowledges. The dream of a simpler, purer Denmark, lovely country by the sea, has passed him by.

He walks, without thinking, toward the voluntary ghetto. He has no intentional heading, only a brief, unpondered sense of wanting to avoid his barren apartment next to the zoo. If he went home, now, what would he do? Sleep, maybe; or eat the miserable remains in his cupboard and then sleep; either way the day would slip by and he would wake tomorrow in his sweaty sheets and take a brief, cold shower and find himself at the hospital again. That would not do, he is sure, though he doesn't really know why. Perhaps it is because people without direction subconsciously seek the last place they knew direction and so Bakman realizes at this late moment that he is walking toward his father's watch shop.

It is boarded up now, of course. After his father's death the shop was closed and the remaining watches sold to relieve debt, to prevent, in his grandmother's words, this particular foolishness from burdening another generation. She had never liked the father, who she considered an intellectual snob who had lured her daughter with pretentious conversation, and she had always taken a not-so-secret pleasure in watching him toil making intricate, meticulously figured timepieces no one would buy. When he died she considered it his just reward, her daughter having already perished from the poor conditions in which he kept his household, unable to afford better; but then she too died shortly after, despite the fact that she cleaned her house with a zealot's passion and ordered her grandson Bakman to give her aging, fleshy body an alcohol bath each night before bed. She would breathe in the heady alcohol fumes and feel them sear her lungs, and whether that hastened her death or kept it an arm's length a week longer no one will know, though Bakman always suspected that she died in order to pursue her adversary, his father, into the afterlife.

After the watch shop was closed the storefront that housed it remained empty. This hadn't been a good area of Copenhagen to start with, which is why his father had been able to rent here, but as the years progressed and the European depression took hold the neighborhood deteriorated even further until it became a refuge for prostitutes and aliens, the outermost ring of Denmark, a place so besotted even the police eliminated it from their routes and any mail intended for those within—little as it was—was simply dropped in the middle of the street and left to its fate.

Bakman looks into the boarded-up shop. Staring in at the place where his father used to repair watches, smelling the familiar odors of ten years previous—for other people this would recall a rush of childhood memories, a sense of what has passed and what is missed. Not Bakman. He has spent so long trying to forget this place that looking into his father's old store is simply that: leaning his head toward the window and looking in. It is an angle from which few people have seen Copenhagen—the unswept sidewalks and brick storefronts of the voluntary ghetto as reflected through one of many dirty windows along this boarded-up street. This is not the Denmark that the German generals, spreading maps of Europe across large oak tables, set out to conquer. But here is, so it must be dealt with. Which is why Bakman sees four German soldiers coming down the street where he is standing.

His first thought is that they are coming for him—well, of course that's his first thought, because he is the kind of man who always thinks a quartet of German soldiers would be coming for him. Or perhaps it's because he's back here, in this neighborhood, that his university degree, his medical schooling, and even his Danish citizenship seem to disappear and he feels like a teenage boy about to be slapped. As they approach—they're smartly dressed in brown, pressed uniforms, and Bakman grows even more aware of the shabbiness of his clothes—he is composing his excuses: I don't know how I got down here, I'm lost, and could you, officers, please direct me home? They're ten feet away now. Bakman shrinks back against the wall, looks down at his feet. They move toward him, heavy batons swinging on one side, leather pistol holsters on the other. Bakman breathes in sharply, closes his eyes.

He feels the German soldiers move past him, down the sidewalk and still in perfect step. He can't help but follow them with his eyes. It only takes a moment before they find who they are looking for. It's none other than the café owner from Nyhaven. Bakman did not come here to find him, but here he is nonetheless. Had he looked around earlier, Bakman would have seen him, only twenty feet further down the sidewalk. He has been living in the voluntary ghetto for six weeks, since his café was closed. Perhaps the café owner had recognized Bakman as well. Perhaps that is why he was walking up the street at the same moment that four German soldiers had been sent here for the express purpose of finding him.

Since the inception of martial law, all packages mailed to Allied countries have been opened and inspected. Two weeks ago the café owner attempted to ship a wedding ring worth a meager fifty kroner and a frame containing a lock of his dead wife's hair to a distant cousin in America. The ring made sense to the German inspector. But the lock of hair? There were few possibilities, one including a coded message of some sort. So the inspector instructed a squad of soldiers attached to German intelligence to find this former café owner with the Jewish name and bring him in for some questions.

He didn't instruct them to be gentle. In three years, when American soldiers in charge of cataloguing German activities in Denmark find the lock of hair, by that time separated from its package, they will look at it once and discard it. But at this moment four German soldiers believe they are hunting down yet another Jew trying to sabotage the Reich. They grab the café owner—whom Bakman now firmly recognizes—and shove him down on his knees, the better to soften him up with one of their batons. Bakman approaches the group, his instinct to run overcome by his sense of recognition. He wants to tap one of the soldiers on the shoulder, explain that there must be some mistake and he, Bakman, has known this man for many years. But in the rush of activity on the dirty street he grabs one of the soldiers by the elbow instead. It's the wrong time to grab a German soldier—as if any good time existed—especially this one, a sergeant who served on the Eastern Front and carries a long scar on his stomach and the memory of near-starvation outside Leningrad. The sergeant has his heavy weapon in his hand, and when he feels the tug at his elbow he turns, assesses the young man in glasses who has grabbed him, and strikes him in the head.

✠ ✠ ✠

After Bothke retreated to his house, Hannah and her mother and father all stood near the doorway, looking out into the street. That man's an idiot, Bergstrom declared. And he's made us late.

Hannah and her father began the walk to the synagogue, a fifteen-minute trip through the quiet streets of Bellahøj into the neighborhood of the university. They spoke little. Twice Bergstrom consulted his watch. Hannah held her dress with one hand as she walked so that its frilled hem would not drag against the stones and the papers in the street.

They had attended synagogue intermittently over the years but Hannah could not recall ever missing a High Holiday service. For much of her childhood she believed that anyone of significance could be found within this synagogue's walls, so much so that when she was ten she begged to bring her next-door neighbor Mari Bothke with them to Rosh Hashanah services. Her parents had been visibly relieved when the elder Bothke refused.

Bergstrom checked his watch again as they crossed out of Bellahøj and descended into Copenhagen proper. He walked more quickly, and Hannah had to hurry to keep up with him. Everything she thought to say felt banal and useless. At least once they arrived at the synagogue she would ascend to the women's section and he would remain downstairs among the masses of *davvening* men and she would have time, finally, to think about what to do next.

Bergstrom opened his watch yet again and shook it, as if it might quit disobeying him and show him the hour and minute he wanted it to display. He was a punctual man. He seemed bothered less by the idea that Bothke could be right—that the Germans were in fact planning an action against all of Jewish Denmark—than by the fact that the man had caused him to be late to a planned appointment.

It was a new year. But what did that mean, really? Hannah could not even name all the months in the Hebrew calendar and the ones that she could—Ab, Tishrei, Kislev—brought to her mind only the vague smell of foreign spices and women dancing as in Esther or Ruth. She wondered if in Jerusalem they marked the days by means of that archaic lunar calendar and she realized how little she knew about the place that had occupied her mind for so many of the last months.

They turned onto Krystalgade and approached the synagogue. It was empty. There was no one in the street and no one in the big courtyard behind the *shul.* They tapped on the door. Nothing. They tapped again. After a while the beadle opened the door. He was old and red-faced and carried ritual objects of every kind. A prayer book peeked out of one pocket and in the other he had jammed three large spice boxes, each worked in filigree and adorned with semiprecious stones. He hugged a Torah scroll with one arm and with the other arm and in both hands he held various ornaments and decorations, all in gold or silver or some fanciful combination of the two. A pomegranate-shaped Torah crown. Finials inscribed with the names of famous cities: Bechhofen, Augsberg, Berlin. A Torah shield that had come to Copenhagen from Lithuania 150 years earlier. In the center of the shield Abraham held a long, curved knife over his son Isaac and small bells hung from its bottom. They jingled as the beadle walked through the door.

Bergstrom asked where everybody was, why the *shul* was empty.

Haven't you heard? the beadle said.

He related that Rosh Hashanah services had not even begun and people were still taking off their coats when the rabbi shouted at everyone to leave. There was a deportation planned, the rabbi announced. Perhaps as soon as that night. The word had come to the rabbi from someone in the German government, an aide or a clerk or some officer, the beadle said. He couldn't remember which. In any case, the rabbi encouraged everyone to make plans to leave Denmark.

To go where? Bergstrom said.

Sweden, the beadle said. Then he began to walk down Krystalgade.

Where are *you* going? Hannah said.

To the church, the beadle said. He tipped his head in the direction of Sankt Petri, a 15th century church near the university. The pastor said he had some room in the basement, the beadle said. Then he plodded away, pausing at a nearby storefront to shift his various burdens. He made a half-hearted attempt to contain it all but there was too much, and some of it just fell into the street.

✠ ✠ ✠

Now the Faeroese walks, across the Knipples Bridge and into Copenhagen. Christianshavn is behind him. He wants to look for her. Already it is dusk and what light there is hangs loosely on the row houses. Buildings stand flat in the shadows as if mere curtains of houses, not real at all, and he walks by them quietly and unnoticed. Pamphlets begin to fall from the sky.

It isn't long before he sees the trucks. They rattle by on the narrow streets, headlights as big as cows' eyes. One stops in front of a doorway and a German steps down from the cab and knocks on the door. No one answers. Other soldiers drop from the back and look into the windows for some sign of inhabitance. Then they all climb back into the truck and it cranks forward with a rough thrusting of the gear stick and stops again, a few doorways down.

He seeks a detail he can build upon, some signal of her habits that will lead to her. When he thinks back to the ghetto now it seems as distant as a memory from his childhood. His sod house, the bare shelves, the sparse outcropping overlooking a desolate and oily sea. He is moving forward again. When he thinks back to the ghetto now all he can remember is disappearance, one face or another vanishing by soldier or starvation or flight. He sees cars moving furtively down the streets, not the Germans now but families in the back seats with their belongings piled on their laps. Then, down other streets, the Germans. They pass within moments of each other like the short life spans of insects. He arrives at Krystalgade, the empty courtyard, a few pamphlets drifting across the stones. Along a far wall a few objects have fallen: a silver pointer shaped like a baby's hand, a few books, a shield of intricate carvings. He picks up the shield and continues walking.

Bergstrom rushed to flag a taxi, which nearly passed them by before grinding to a stop in the narrow street. The taxi driver claimed a 50% surcharge to pay for gas under martial law; Bergstrom handed it over, though not without complaint. Hannah looked out the window at the row houses as they sped by, and she and Bergstrom spoke little. They saw no Germans.

Though she had rehearsed in her mind the process of leaving Denmark, she still did not know what to expect from the next few hours. She had imagined this departure so many times—the dream had occupied her nearly every day of that summer—but in each instance the thought had been bookended by a desired destination, the arrival on a kibbutz or in some small town in Palestine. That was part of it, a necessary part. Now she was being forced to go. As the taxi drove toward Bellahøj she felt Copenhagen taking on a new degree of color and desire. She longed for every small shop, worn street, flower seller, newspaper stand, places only a week earlier she would gladly have put behind her and never seen again.

They arrived at the house and found her mother sitting in the dark at the dining room table. She had put all the foods out, and they were arrayed in bowls and on the china plates like offerings at the Temple.

A man was here, her mother said quietly.

What do you mean? Bergstrom asked. Was it a . . . ?

No. A man from the hospital. A doctor, I think. He said he was with the resistance. He was walking up and down the streets looking for doors with Jewish nameplates. Also stopping at each door with a *mezuzah*. You should consider taking that down, he said. If you're ever able to return here.

He told me that a car would come by this neighborhood later tonight, her mother continued. We should get in it, he said.

For what?

The car will take us up north, he said. We can hide there until we can arrange to go to Sweden.

This is ridiculous, Bergstrom said. I've had enough of this. We're not getting in any car. Who was this man?

Hannah watched as her mother picked up one of the plates from the table. It held an entire quartered chicken, the skin still warm from the oven. She threw the plate against the wall, shattering it and leaving a greasy stain on the floral wallpaper. It was quieter than Hannah would have thought.

Sarah! Bergstrom said.

Her mother picked up another plate, slung it against the far wall. Bergstrom jumped back as she threw it. It split against the wall and the pieces fell to the floor. Then she wiped her hand on the tablecloth.

What are you doing? Bergstrom said.

When the car comes, we will get in it, her mother said.

Hannah bent to pick up the pieces of plate.

Leave it! her mother hissed. Go upstairs and pack a bag. Bring your jewelry.

When Hannah came down from her room twenty minutes later, she found her father standing in front of their china closet. He turned a single teacup over in his hand.

I could have sold this, he said. I could have sold all of this.

He had pushed the food for Rosh Hashanah dinner to one side and had stacked on the table all of the belongings he could claim as valuable. He had divided them into two piles. What he would sell, if needed, and what he wouldn't. On the left, three watches, a gold pen, a group of carvings in ivory and jade. On the right, his wife's jewelry. After a moment he took some of the jewelry and moved it to the left. He pointed to the pile on the right and said, This is what we'll keep. But Hannah thought, No, on the left is what you'll sell first. On the right is what you'll sell next.

They heard the honk of a horn and Bergstrom put his face to the window. Is that it? he said.

They went outside with their five suitcases. A truck idled on the side of the road. It was old and rode low to the ground. The bed of the truck had high walls and there was a thick canvas tarp to cover the back, along with a few crates of potatoes. If anything they could crawl under the tarp and they would look like a load of vegetables.

The three Bergstroms stood by the truck with their bags there in the street. Another couple was also walking toward the car, dragging a large suitcase behind them. The woman walked, the man dragged. Hannah knew their faces from the neighborhood but didn't recognize them as Jewish. Indeed it turned out only the woman was. I'm staying here, the man said, to no one in particular. Hannah looked over to the Bothke house for some sign of her friend Mari but the windows were dark.

Don't tell me your names, the driver said. I don't want to know them. Then they climbed in the truck and were soon riding out of Copenhagen.

18

soldiers, or the possibility of

Bakman wakes to Henrik standing over him, poking and prodding in what feels like, to Bakman, a dramatic and excessive manner. He reaches to his head, which seems all right except for a knobby bump over his temple. Also, there's something wrong with his glasses, or his left eye, he's not sure which, because Henrik is fuzzy on that side, like a train disappearing off the side of a movie screen. The whole thing's cinematic, really, except that instead of concern for the characters he's feeling actual, grinding pain in his head, which would be quite an accomplishment, even for a film, a medium for which Bakman has the highest regard. He'd like to see more films really, but he hasn't got the time, which he suddenly remembers is mostly because he's in the resistance and he's just been brutally attacked by a German.

We almost lost you there, Henrik says.

More dramatic and excessive patting. Bakman would sure like to know where he is. Maybe Henrik will tell him. He asks, though it's hard to know if he's said it out loud.

Typical Bakman, Henrik says. Always a little flighty. You remember back in school when they let us go outside for lunch? You would wander around in the grass and forget to come back to class unless I retrieved you.

That's true, Bakman thinks, though in his version, Henrik called him over, then pulled Bakman's sweater over his head to blind him before shoving him into a thicket of brambles. Leaving Bakman to shout for help until some teacher came to look for him. And would Henrik please please please stop patting him?

Just performing my physician's duty, Henrik says. You took quite a tumble, you know. A lesser physician might have lost you. Head wounds can be so tricky.

Bakman still can't see very well, so he has begun to feel around the space to his right. There's a lot to be learned by exploring the world this way, as he now discovers. For example, the floor beneath him is cold and tiled. Moving up from there it's a bit warmer, with just the tiniest little bubbles of paint. The wall. He'd like to examine the textures to his left, but that hand is occupied with some gauze Henrik has placed in it and every time he tries to move it from his head it returns as if tethered by a pulley.

You're an unhelpful patient, Henrik says. Please keep that dressing to your head. I'm committed to stabilizing your fluctuating health, but it'll go a lot easier on both of us if you'd exert a little pressure.

Bakman feels someone push on the back of his left hand. That's better, Henrik says.

There are probably some recollections that could account for his current situation, if only he could put them in sequence. He remembers a German soldier, but when he concentrates on that it just increases the vicious pounding over his left eye. The gauze is getting sticky. Wasn't he talking to the café owner?

Typical Bakman, Henrik says. Didn't Henrik say that before?

There's practically an entire revolt going on, and you're talking about having coffee, Henrik says.

Henrik has now begun to disappear and reappear although his words remain with only a slight rearrangement of sound. Bakman is starting to put together more of his most recent memories, beginning at the point when the German bashed him over the head. He'd never been hit like that before. He'd happily file it under new experience if there wasn't so much pain involved.

I already gave you something for the pain, Henrik says. I'd give you more, but then you wouldn't be able to do your solemn duty to our lovely country. And I know you'll thank me later for keeping you in the game.

It's all making a good deal more sense to Bakman now, including that initial episode with the man with the hole in his side. Resistance all along.

Bakman wonders if it's actually too late to undamage his head and generally rearrange the last four months of his life. He's beginning to find his destination troubling.

We don't have much time now, Henrik says. The Germans will be here soon. And they'll be looking for our new friends.

Bakman would like to ask who these new friends are, but the smell where he's sitting has become familiar. Like a pickle soaked in chemicals. The morgue. His morgue.

If I'd known you felt so proprietary about it, Henrik says, I'd have asked your permission before inviting everyone else.

The recognition of odors has somehow brought his vision back into play, and though the lights are dim he can discern a number of shadows playing around the tables and the floor. They're Jews. And they're looking at him.

The possibility is occurring to Bakman that the immediate future might involve his getting shot. Henrik has made his task clear. He's supposed to go upstairs and look for Germans. Bakman is desperate for another hour to go by, because then, according to Henrik, the Jews will leave his morgue and his hospital and his city and he'll be free of all Jewish matters entirely. Still, couldn't they all vacate his morgue right now, so that he could lie down on one of the wide, cold tables and take a nap, after which he'd happily readjust his head bandage and help the Jews go wherever Henrik wanted?

He had already done plenty. He had traveled up to that dull and depressing fishing town, hadn't he, and now he was being asked to serve as a lookout while these Jews tried to escape the hospital. It's a decent plan, though it holds some pretty small distinctions for him. He tries to explain this to Henrik, who in his usual obstinate way fails to catch any of the finer points of Bakman's argument. It goes like this: Whatever happens next, the end result is the same—no Jews.

What are you talking about? Henrik says. They are standing in the hallway now, a narrow corridor with three doorways. On the other side of the morgue door are forty people, half of them dead bodies and the other half Jews. Above, on the first floor of the hospital, are German soldiers, or the possibility of German soldiers. At the moment it seems about the same to Bakman.

They'll be gone, Bakman says. Either way they'll be gone. If the Germans pile them in trucks and take them away there will be no more Jews here. If we stuff them into fishing boats and send them to Sweden there will be no Jews here. Don't you see? Bakman lowers his voice, conscious that he is speaking of people standing just on the other side of a thin door. Either way they'll be gone.

That, Henrik says, is the stupidest thing I've ever heard.

Maybe, Bakman responds. He has come around to thinking that getting bashed in the head had its benefits. Certain elements seem clearer now. He pauses for a moment, trying to locate a particular thought. It seems to linger just outside his realm of focus. A-ha! he continues, pointing a finger at Henrik. This is it. Either way, it's not going to be very much fun for them.

You're ridiculous. I've tolerated it this far because we're friends, and you've recently taken some damage to your skull. But you better get up there and do your job. People are depending on you.

Bakman likes the note of desperation in Henrik's voice. People are depending on him, at least Henrik is, and if Bakman doesn't go up there and distract some Germans,

Henrik is going to be screwed. Positively fucked. I'll do it, he says to Henrik. But only because I want to.

He likes this. After this whole episode is over, things are going to be different. He likes it very much.

Yes, Bakman thinks, I'll go up there and distract some Germans. He doesn't think of himself as inherently distracting, but maybe with some effort. He doesn't know any dances, and as far as conversation, he'd always found himself lacking for words during terrifying situations. Still, he likes the idea of it. Let Henrik stay down here and guard my morgue. I'm in charge now.

He checks his dressing in the reflection of the glass on a door. Henrik has wrapped the dressing in a slant from his hairline to his left eyebrow. Dried blood has soaked through and the bandage has pushed up his hair in the manner of a mental patient. It is all a bit indistinct since the bandage covers most of his left eye and the lens on that side of his glasses has broken or fallen out anyway. Well, he thinks, this should help in the distraction department.

As he climbs the stairs it occurs to him that there might not be any Germans up there. He doesn't put it past Henrik to overinflate the whole situation, drag all those people from their homes with their suitcases and make them share space with dead bodies just on some romantic whim. That would be like Henrik. He says he is a member of the resistance, but does Bakman have any independent confirmation of that? It could all be circumstantial, the man who was killed in the explosion, the trip up to Gilleleje—who did Bakman tell about that anyway? only Henrik. Had he,

Bakman, witnessed any acts of resistance? No, no, no. And who was Henrik, anyway? Just some medical student, like himself, no important person, not in the larger scheme, and who did he think he was to make all those people sit in a morgue?

But when Bakman gets to the top of the stairs he finds the main lobby of the hospital full of German soldiers. The sight of them makes his head ache all over again. Their dark uniforms stand out against the eggshell hospital walls. There's a group of them surrounding the receptionist's desk like a cloud of carrion birds. Others wait in the corridor, inspecting their rifles. One smokes a cigarette.

Bakman stops a nurse. She tries to shrug him off, thinking he's a wandering patient, but he holds on to her until she recognizes him.

What do they want? he asks.

They're searching the hospital. They came here to question people. I don't know who. I think they're looking for Jews.

That's it? Bakman says.

They also say some people in this hospital are active in the resistance and they want to speak to them. They say they don't want to arrest anyone. Just talk to them. But I don't believe it.

Do you speak German? he says.

What?

Do you speak German?

A little. I guess I do.

Tell them it's me.

What?

Tell them it's me. Tell them I'm the resistance leader here.

You? But you're nobody.

He lets go of her with a shove. Fine, he says. I'll tell them myself.

He walks by a cart holding tape, an I.V. bag, syringes, a cup of water. He takes the cup of water. A German officer, a captain, is leaning over the receptionist's desk to look at some paperwork. Bakman walks at the group of soldiers, passing by several as he heads toward their leader. The cup is shaking in his hand. He stops next to the captain, who turns to look at him. Bakman takes the cup of water and splashes it into the captain's face.

Come get me, he says.

And he runs.

They're following him, all in a line, the German soldiers, because that's what they're trained to do. He sprints down the hallway and they follow, boots and rifles clicking like mandibles. He's ahead by a few steps, all the soldiers in a line behind him, or so he thinks, since he doesn't know that they're also trained to branch out into a pincer approach, a studied and tested series of maneuvers involving flanking and rotating and minute adjustments in position aiming for maximum advantage, and how could the Germans clear entire ghettos and towns if they don't know how to outmaneuver one clumsy-footed medical student? But he'll find out soon enough.

He swivels down a short passage and pivots up a staircase, gaining a couple of seconds by knowing the hospital.

He's thinking that he's doing a pretty good job with this, especially considering the head wound. He's thinking also, as he runs, that the next time he douses a German captain with water he'd better be more prepared, take steps veteran resistance members probably already know, like tying your shoes tightly and effectively. He's thinking this because as he runs his right shoe is beginning to slip off at the heel, which is a distraction that he'll just have to put up with at this point. He thinks also that despite whatever academic training a person could accumulate in resistance activities there's probably no substitute for practical experience, which he's getting right now, and would you know you were do something important for your county until you were in the middle of it, and how could you be sure even then?

He reaches the fifth floor and takes off down the hallway, the patients all staring at him from their rooms, which he enjoys, knowing how their puzzled looks will translate to shock when they see the soldiers, and he's also thinking how he's never run before with no further object in mind, he's not running to *get anywhere*, after all, just running to delay what now seems like an inevitable conclusion as he nears the end of the hallway, that he'll get caught, but hopefully in the minutes or half-minutes or few more seconds between now and then something positive will happen involving those people in his morgue. And so he runs. There's a doorway at the end of the hall, or maybe a window. He can hear the soldiers coming out of the stairwell behind him. He's running hard to the end now, and as he gets close he can see it's just a big window, no escape, but there doesn't seem to be a great point in stopping, so he carries straight through it, and then he's falling.

Now in a truck, the shield clattering against his chest. The Faeroese taps it once to test its sound. It clinks like a tin can, for all its brilliance.

The driver beside him is talking, a short man with a wide, powerful chest. The driver gestures at Copenhagen outside the windshield, his left hand fluttering declensions of unhappiness at the state of his city.

This truck had driven by when he was standing outside the synagogue. A quick wave from the driver, the door swinging open. Then they were negotiating the streets of the city, the truck swinging hard against each turn, the driver honking at startled pedestrians.

What they had seen. On the streets driving out of Copenhagen, past the big building, the hospital. A man flew out of a window on the hospital's top floor, clawing the air in hard, bitter swipes. The driver braked the truck to look. When the soldiers came out of the hospital they prodded the body with rifles, boots. The driver shook his head and aimed the truck to Gilleleje. Papers fell from the sky.

Now tunneling along inland roads, barns and fields passing like a thought against the darkness. Soon they are at the sea again, he knows it, feels the dampness in his clothes. The smell old and familiar. The truck pulls up to the boats, scattering people in its path. Rasps to a stop. The driver shoos him out of the cab, laughs. Then drives away, back to the city of so recent disappointment.

19

the rumor of money

When the pastor gathered them in the church all the men stood about. They had little to say. There would be payments for their services, individually negotiated. Poul Andersen said, I'll be taking my boat out anyway tonight. Won't hurt me to have a little company. Several of the men laughed, embarrassed.

Of course Carl's back hurts him terribly now. Why should this evening be different than any other? He had warmed it at home, next to their stove, but it has tightened again in the cold night air, as if corroded by salt.

There are Jews outside the church, whole families and their luggage. Eyes averted, waiting for the doors to open.

Carl leaves out a back door to check his boat. When he arrives he finds Jette standing over the engine. She has in her hands a long sledgehammer, half as tall as herself, shared by the fishermen to flatten metal or break open a rusted chain. She holds it over the exposed engine, trying to find the balance that will allow her to drive the heavy end against the motor of Carl's boat. When Carl comes upon her she doesn't look surprised, only continues to balance the hammer over the exposed engine.

He sits down next to her. I can't go anyway, he says.

The Bergstroms moved out reluctantly from the truck, dragging their suitcases. Nothing but open space between themselves and the fishing docks, no obvious place to hide. Hannah's father looked down the road for any sign of German vehicles. There was a large church down the shore, a few fishing boats ahead, and past that, nothing but lapping water. If Sweden were out there ready to welcome them, Hannah could not see it. She could only trust the locals of this town, people she had never met or set eyes on before and whose first and family names remained a mystery.

They had all of them entered a crude bargaining for the buying of passage. The travelers stood dressed in fine clothes, the men in suits and the women in sober dresses and they carried luggage designed for a much better class of travel than the one that lay ahead of them. The Bergstroms' own luggage had been bought before the war for vacation on a ferry to Bornholm, and it still bore the crested tags of that grand ship.

There seemed no one in charge, only a general understanding that certain people needed to leave and other people needed to take them. They won't let us bring all these things, her father said. Look at these small boats.

So her mother opened their suitcases there on the dock, giving all the other families a view of their shirts, hats, underclothes. This is not a thing my mother would ever have done before, Hannah thought. But she's doing it now. Her mother pulled out shoes and, measuring them against the feet of people standing by, handed them out. Silks from Copenhagen merchants. Hand-stitched blouses. All given away to fishermen and fishermen's wives. Her family pictures she pulled from their frames and repacked against the flat end of a suitcase. The frames she left on the ground, empty.

When Hannah looked up from that she saw her father speaking to a fisherman and his wife. Money passed between them, bills of variant denominations, and Hannah tried to count them but she couldn't wrap her mind around the task. She tried to count the individual bills as they sat in the fisherman's hand but she couldn't keep track of numbers. It could have been anything. The bills sat openhanded in the fisherman's palm so that if a brisk wind had arrived it would have scattered them about the dock and the water and amongst the discarded luggage, leaving just the rumor of money in the fisherman's hand. After a time the fisherman handed the bills to his wife, still not closing his hand on them, and she took the money and folded it and tucked it down the front of her blouse like Hannah had seen in a country grocery many years ago.

Then the man and his wife began to prepare their boat. Other fishermen were doing the same and Hannah would have thought they would help each other but they did not. They worked in blind imitation of each other, coiling ropes, spreading nets, counting items Hannah did not even have names for. One fisherman called to another for a type of wrench and that fisherman produced it from amongst the spaces of his boat. The man needing the wrench was three vessels down the pier and so the wrench owner handed it to a Jew standing by his boat. That Jew in turn passed it to the next who passed it to the next until it reached the far boat. Each man who took it did so wordlessly and passed it with two open hands to the next. They looked like men passing a dish at a church dinner. When the wrench reached its destination the fisherman took it and bent into his boat like such sequences were a feature of his everyday life.

Around Hannah people began handing their belongings down to the small boats. The pastor enlisted two fishermen's sons to stand as lookouts at the train station and on the Copenhagen road. One Jew approached his assigned boat with one hand carrying his luggage and the other pushing his bicycle. He paid his money and then demanded that his bicycle be given passage as well. He said he needed it in Sweden, though whether his motive was economic or sentimental Hannah could not determine. It seemed like just an ordinary bicycle with a wooden box on the front.

Could the fisherman vouch for the bicycles in Sweden? he asked. Maybe everyone in that country went about clod-footed and slowly.

When the fisherman refused the man tried to push it himself onto the fishing boat, though no one else would help him and alone he could not manage the contrary movements of the bicycle wheel and boat, dock and tide. Finally the fisherman climbed up out of his boat and grabbed the bicycle from the man's hands. He hoisted it onto his shoulder and carried it behind a nearby storehouse, where he dumped it on a pile of garbage and fish carcasses. The man shouted at the fisherman and at two others nearby and then sat down on a wooden pylon, holding his head. He kicked at a seagull, which flapped a few feet away and then strutted right back at his feet.

The scene made Hannah think of a story she had heard as a child, David crying for his lost Absalom, except this man was just a man and his beloved a bicycle. She held her own suitcase on her lap, imagining it thrown on one of many garbage heaps and stinking of fish bones.

A few minutes later the bicycle man was standing again in front of the fishing boat. He had discarded his suitcase and carried just the spoked rear wheel of his prized bicycle under his arm, as if it might form the basis for another bicycle in Sweden, or failing that, serve as a tool for memory in that country he hoped to reach.

The itinerant pastor moved among these families as they waited, offering words of encouragement, condolence, calm. They just had to wait until dark, the pastor said. Once they were on the water they would be in Sweden and gone from this trouble forever. This did not balm their waiting as the pastor might have hoped; the mention of their destination only suggested how much they were leaving behind. They began to mill about again, having lost some of their stunned quality.

Hannah had never in all her life so wished for a task to occupy her. She had none. Instead she watched the fisherman and his wife prepare their boat. They made adjustments to the engine and unwrapped the hawsers until only two thin lines fastened the boat to the pier. As the man and woman worked, every act seemed a kindness to Hannah, and she wanted to stop them and praise them for each individual motion. The fisherman, blond and worn but still broad-chested, moved slowly, laboring under a burden Hannah could not identify.

Finally they were ready to board. The fisherman brought out an armload of cod from one of the storehouses and threw it across the front half of the boat, onto a canvas tarp. Her father got in first, teetering as the boat shied under his weight. Then he held out his hands for her mother. She bunched her skirt and as she stepped over the bow Hannah saw a glimpse of her mother's calf, white, like the underbellies of the fish that waited to share the boat with them.

Hannah thought of the truck she and Aaron had sent through Germany, the girl who had cried and been consoled, and Hannah wished for someone to wave her off from the dock. There was no one, however. Nearly everyone in her Zionist group was dead.

Her mother and father lifted the heavy tarp of fish and slid under it as they might descend under bedcovers. The luggage they kicked down to the foot of the tarp with their feet. As Hannah readied herself to step in the boat, she heard the pastor shout, then the bleating of a horn and the screeching of heavy tires. She turned back to see people scattering in the wake of a truck.

This looks like one of yours, she hears the truck driver say, thumbing his right hand toward someone in the cab. Can you believe it. He's standing there in the square holding this shiny thing in front of him like a sign that says *Arrest me.* Not much for conversation, either. But I figure you'll know what to do with him. And with that pulls away, leaving the Faeroese standing among the Jews, the ridiculous Torah shield hung around his neck. He looked at Hannah.

1942

In the scarce week before he had left for Copenhagen the entire town of Kotlum, northern Faeroe Islands, had fallen into a savage and desperate whale hunt. The first whale spotted was a young and obviously daft one, for it wandered into the harbor immune to the ghosts of previous generations of dead creatures. Older whales followed, their experience marked in gouges and pits across their rubberized skin. The young whale possessed a sleek, water-plowing shape and it looked up at the wooden longboat with bright cetaceous eyes as a harpoon was aimed at its forehead.

The harpoonist was an uncle of the Faeroese, and had struck out into the cove prepared with just a small cod net. He carried in his worn longboat a small, handheld version of a harpoon, no more than a barbed dart lashed to a doorknob. The blade itself carved from a toothbrush handle. Apparently it did the job, though, for it plunged into the brain matter with little resistance and sank to the nub. The whale swooned and died. His uncle leaned over the side of the boat and watched the whale sink to the floor of the cove, which was shallow, since his boat was not yet thirty feet from the shoreline.

When the uncle looked up from that evident sight he saw the water swollen with whales. They filled the cove like a bathtub. With no other signal available, he pulled off his oilcloth jacket and waved it above his head and shouted.

The cove at Kotlum was bent like a half-moon, open to the north. Fierce cliffs guarded the entrance at either side, and lines of jagged rock studded the water throughout. At the base of the cove a small batch of dwellings had broken out, with moorings for twenty boats. Some of the structures stood no bigger than an icebox. They seemed altogether unlikely structures, though they had stood there, some of them, for hundreds of years.

The Faeroe Islander's own house sat on a naked plain above the cove. Like elsewhere on the island the site did not offer root-bearing holds for much more than a fern. Still, at a run, it took less than a full minute to move from paring his nails in his damp house to pulling his boat into the water.

By the time he arrived most of the island's small population was occupied with various stages of whale-killing. Women gathered on the hill above the cove and set out blankets to watch. The men stove out toward the whales in boats of all sizes and conditions, some leaking near as much water as they kept out. His own boat was mostly tar, and bubbled where water sloshed between its layers. He brought two harpoons, which was fortunate, since one broke almost immediately and it took several tries for him to kill his first whale. After that he slew several, for he had long ago discovered his talent at such an act.

Soon the slaughter became widespread. Three men abandoned all pretense of boats and, half-lunging through the bracing water, chased whales. He saw a man, armed with only a pocketknife, stabbing a whale from dorsal fin to fluke, until the animal seemed to die of simple exhaustion. The man continued to jab at it in a numbed, repeated manner, like a grocer determined to reduce an ice block to mere shavings.

The water had become greasy with blood. The whole event lay before him. The men dragged carcasses to the shore and stood about and inspected them. One man crawled head first inside a whale, Jonah-like, examining he knew not what. When the cove grew bluish with darkness they lit fires of fresh whale oil and continued to work. They torched an entire half of a whale, and its fat bubbled and then it caught to a raging blaze like it possessed rivers of oil in its capillaries. They stood around it like a bonfire, and it had all the features of a simpler time.

When he had finished dividing a small whale he looked at its bones as if he might read signs in their arrangement, some fortune in the relationship of its parts. But it was a dead thing now, without signal or message, defined only by stillness.

When he boarded the boat at Tórshavn a week later his pants still hung stiff below the knees. When he worked his feet in his boots he discovered fresh pockets of dampness.

21

a house built for the sea

Could he have returned their money, he would have. It already felt like a scolding weight in his pocket. Go home, Carl wanted to say. Take your fate. But Jette climbed into the boat and took the wheel in her hands. Carl threw off the lines and cast them at her feet. Even that exhausted him. Wait for me, she called back to him. He watched as she followed the other boats into the cold and unforgiving Sound.

Dampness in the narrow boat, the tarp heavy with fish-weight on top of her. The boards underneath offer little protection from the frigid water. It laps at her back. She reaches out to her mother and father, barely moving, to her right. To the left, also hidden under the tarp, is the man in the fishing sweater. He had slipped into the boat as they cast off, wordless as ever.

Hannah feels no reassurance, no progress, from the scratching of the waves and the rasp of the boat's small engine. With a forefinger she pushes down a corner of the tarp but all that reveals is the staring eye of a cod, right in her face. Then the boat shudders around her and she hears a motor grinding toward them. She pulls the tarp back over her face and curls against the boards.

When the German patrol boat pulls up through the fog Jette knows that she is alone, exposed. They have reached only halfway between Denmark and Sweden. She tries to gather her hair up but it makes a crude disguise. She cannot imitate a man, cannot pass for an innocent fisherman. The patrol boat is steered right alongside, its searchlight blinding her and roaming over the boat. She blinks then, sees there are two of them aiming their rifles. When they wave at her to shut her engine, she presses her hand over the throttle and the *Jette* goes silent.

Only in the last hour of the whale hunt had he begun to tire, his arms worn with slicing and cutting the rubbery outer skin, his blade edge catching repeatedly on the bones. Night had descended all through the cove and his hands so bloody that the knife slipped loose and he had to pull it out of the folds of blubber. He remembers now the warmth inside the whale's body, a house built for the sea, a body in motion, moving, moving, until it meets the harpoon.

It is with this desire that he reaches for the two young German soldiers in front of him, crossing the distance between the boats with a sturdy leap, one he has brought all the way from his childhood. He would jump from boat to boat in the cove, the water passing beneath him then as it does now, even as they swing their rifles at him.

He jumps toward them as if he wishes to tell them something. There are things he has seen, the crashed pilot, the still whale, his brothers drowned, his mother bleeding from glass nabbed into her wrist, a young woman with hair like a crow's bristles, and he wishes to tell all this to the two men so he jumps. When he hits the deck of the patrol boat it tilts with his weight and the rolling of the sea, he reaches out to embrace them, and he carries them like his own brothers into the freezing water.

The *Jette* lurches into motion again, straining against the waves, its bow bobbing and tipping. The tarp falls away, and Hannah catches a cold breath of the night air. She lifts her head and sees the patrol boat drifting behind them.

Put the boat lamp on, Hannah says to the blond woman.

I can't put it on, the woman replies. We have to go now.

What happened? Hannah says, but the woman doesn't answer. She has her head down and Hannah thinks she hears crying. Her parents rustle under the tarp as if in restless sleep. It is the first, greyish tint of the morning. Hannah can see a shoreline growing more distinct in regular increments, and in the fog and weak light she can only trust that it is Sweden.

By four in the morning Carl was walking to the beach, tramping through the high grass, passing by the church and feeling the straw shoots grow thinner and thinner under his feet until they gave way to sand and harsh rocks.

He looked out into the Sound. All he could see were grey waves, heavy with fog. They broke against the beach and slid away.

At the docks, the pastor had pleaded with the fishermen's wives to disperse, for their safety and the safety of those out on the water. One by one they left to wait out the evening at home. A polite rain began to fall.

You too, the pastor said to Carl.

I can't go home.

Then go somewhere else, the pastor said. Please, he added.

Carl walked away, rubbing his back. He didn't care what the pastor thought of him; in any case, he could not go home. He decided to walk down the shore to where he would be the first to see the blue-hulled boats return.

The rocks at the beach were sharp and unyielding and beset by a festering moss. This moss would wither and die over the coming winter, Carl knew, leaving rocks as bleached as old bones.

He hated the water. Had always hated it. Let the wives and the pastor think what they will: that he had shied away from his boat because his back hurt or worse, because he was a coward.

He had never talked to God and so he had a hard time getting started. First he just stood there. Then he said: If you bring her back to me . . . He paused to find a more measured tone. Then he said: When you bring her back to me, I will crack the *Jette* into a hundred small, broken boards and never go out into that water again. I will litter this beach with the pieces.

He looked around for someone to stand as his witness but he was alone so he looked over his shoulder to the church and decided that would have to be sufficient. He turned back to the beach. There was a long dark shape at the edge of the water, just a few dozen feet from where he stood.

Carl knew what he had found. He had seen dead men before, of course. Carl was very, very tired, and his thoughts had begun to swim together. The man with the dark hair and a torn, black fisherman's sweater. The man who had crossed on his boat. The strange breastplate still hung from his neck and over his chest and right arm.

Carl pushed at him with his boot. The man was light, as if he had just expelled all his breath. He had probably died in the waves just a few feet from the shore.

Having waited seven hours, Carl was now left with a dead man for company. He wished to wait no longer. He reached down to the Faeroese's wet shoulders and began to pull.

This is going to hurt, he thought. But not more than I deserve.

Carl pulled the man up the gravel road toward the church and the breastplate clattered and the man's boots dragged in the road. It sounded like dripping water. Carl passed a house along the road and wondered what he would say if someone came out and saw him and this dead man, but no one came out and Carl said nothing.

It took a long time to drag the body up the hill next to the church. He looked at the scene on the breastplate, a man holding a knife to a young boy's throat, unaware of the ram in the thicket beside them. Several times Carl paused and scouted the sea. Nothing.

He would go. If Jette would come back out of the fog and return from Sweden he would pack up their belongings and board the train with her to Copenhagen. The money in his pocket would give them a start. They would find an apartment near his sister-in-law and her husband and Carl would take a job fixing boats. He would sit in a chair and tap on a boat engine with his wrench and periodically say, This one looks all right.

And if she did not return he would go anyway. He would arrive at his sister-in-law's bearing a small suitcase and the memory of his wife and would sit at their kitchen table and drink with the husband and say little for many days. Then he would go out and buy presents for his nephews and niece and keep company with the husband. He would wait for the war to end and grow into a strange old man. Which he might anyway.

By the time he reached the Viking graveyard with the dead man the houses of Gilleleje had begun to appear in the morning light. Carl's clothes hung damp with sweat. The ground was soft and on his hands and knees and with the help of a flat stone he was able to dig a shallow grave. Layers of sod and grass gathered in heaps where he worked. When he was done he had a trench, a wound in the ground. He arranged the stones and pushed in the body and covered it. Then he tamped down the dirt over the eighteenth Viking grave, facing east.

Epilogue

In the first year in Sweden they moved five times, traveling like pilgrims seeking destinations ever farther from the sea. Her father used his poor Swedish to sell hosiery door-to-door among the cold logging towns of the north. He would be gone for weeks at a time. The news of Copenhagen and her father's factory grew more and more vague over time, so that by summer 1945, two years after their escape, he didn't know whether he would find even an empty shell of his mill when he returned.

Still, her parents were surprised when, at the war's end, Hannah didn't board the celebratory boat back to Copenhagen but instead descended into Germany. She volunteered in displaced persons' camps, trying to revive the skeletal Eastern European survivors who died at an alarming rate. By then the occupation of Germany was complete, and as Hannah walked through the burnt and depressed German towns the grim faces of the locals made her think often of Copenhagen.

In the early spring of 1947, in southern France, she boarded a cargo ship that had been built in Baltimore,

Maryland, and had been refitted as a crude passenger carrier. In the middle of the night a man painted on it a name, *Exodus.* They set sail under cover of grey clouds for Jerusalem.

She sweated through two days in the ship's fetid hold, eating only stiff bread and an orange subdivided among the nearest seven people. Past Cyprus, the ship stopped when confronted by six British destroyers. By megaphone, the captain of the flag warship announced that recent unrest prohibited any immigration to Palestine, now or for the foreseeable future. Hannah climbed to the ship's deck and looked to the east, where she could see the Arab city of Ashkelon on the coast. The *Exodus* tried to move forward despite the warning. British troops boarded in a stately and organized manner. They proceeded to beat Jews. Hannah struggled toward the stern to escape suffocation in the crowds. After five hours of sporadic fighting two British soldiers fired into a group that had surrounded them. Three refugees died instantly and many more were crushed as people fled below decks from the riot.

From her place at the stern Hannah looked over the rail and saw a man, his bloody arm bound up in a crude sling, climb out a porthole and fall into the churning water. He vanished, then resurfaced and began to swim. He paddled in uneven strokes, encumbered by the sling. A fishing boat motored out from shore to try to retrieve him, but drew fire from a British ship and was forced to retreat. Hannah watched as a crude kind of game gathered for judging the immediacy of the man's drowning, and those who weighed in with an early number won.

The British forced the boat back to France, where it sat in the harbor for days as those aboard refused to get off. Then the British steered it around West Europe to Hamburg, an insulting journey, as Hannah fought off a fever and a woman gave birth in the dark just a few feet away. Once at Hamburg the British pried the refugees loose from the handrails and dumped them, by the hundreds, onto the German shore.

She tried again. She boarded a boat that made it all the way into the harbor of Tel Aviv, bearing a sign rendered into meticulous English: THE GERMANS DESTROYED OUR FAMILIES AND HOMES. DON'T YOU DESTROY OUR HOPES. The British sent it back to Europe. She tried again.

On her third attempt she entered Palestine through the northern port of Akko, on a small boat posing as an Arab fishing trawler. Once again entering a country in disguise. She traveled once through Petaq Tiqva, the desert town mentioned in Sofie's letter of nine years before, and found it so different from her imagining that she concluded her business there quickly and avoided it from then on. When the war came, Hannah took residence at a moshav north of Tel Aviv. She packed ammunition and handed it to men who went out and died with it. She heard the proclamation of the State on a tinny radio and went to bed that night with a man who had chased Arab women from their village with a stick.

After the war she settled at Kibbutz Lochmai ha-Ghettaot, the Ghetto Fighters' Kibbutz. She married an American and gave birth to children with pretty Hebrew names. She was happy. She felt distant, though, from the other kibbutzniks, so many of whom had survived the brutal liquidation of Warsaw. Had, by their own hand, killed Germans with bombs made from liquor-filled bottles. They held close to themselves, Hannah thought, this great, indelible, heart-filling moment, while she could not explain to them or to herself all the small things that had brought her to this place.